SNOWED IN WITH YOU

JADE CHURCH

Serendipity, 51 Gower Street, London, WC1E 6HJ
info@serendipityfiction.com | www.serendipityfiction.com

© Jade Church, 2024

The right of the above author to be identified as the author of this work has been asserted in accordance with the Copyright, Designs and Patents Act 1988. British Library Cataloguing in Publication Data available.

Print ISBN: 978-1-7398968-0-5
Ebook ISBN: 978-1-7398968-1-2

Set in Times.
Cover design by Ditte Løekkegaard.

All characters, other than those clearly in the public domain, and place names, other than those well-established such as towns and cities, are fictitious and any resemblance is purely coincidental.

All rights reserved. No part of this publication may be reproduced, stored in or introduced into a retrieval system, or transmitted, in any form, or by any means electronic, mechanical, photocopying, recording or otherwise, without the prior permission of the publisher. Any person who commits any unauthorised act in relation to this publication may be liable to criminal prosecution and civil claims for damages.

Jade Church is an avid reader and writer of spicy romance. She loves sweet and swoony love interests who aren't scared to smack your ass and bold female leads. Jade currently lives in the U.K. and spends the majority of her time reading and writing books, as well as binge re-watching The Vampire Diaries.

You can follow Jade Church on social media:

Website: jadechurchauthor.com

Instagram handle: @authorjadechurch

TikTok: @authorjadechurch

Also by this author

TEMPER THE FLAME

PROLOGUE

SARA

The moment the last two months had been leading to arrived to applause and cheers as the newlyweds walked into the reception hall in time to the music. I was already three glasses of champagne deep into the night so my claps might have been a little sloppier than that of the groomsman next to me, Fletcher. But to be fair, I had helped plan this wedding, so I should definitely get to enjoy it now. I'd flown out to California to stay with my brother, Robert, and his fiancé-now-wife, Tanya. It had been... bearable. Mostly. Tanya was a sweetheart and I'd been glad to have the chance to get to know her properly before the wedding, as well as offer her an escape if she got cold feet about marrying Rob. I loved my brother, but God was he an ass.

'They look so happy,' Fletcher said, a giant smile on his face that sent butterflies flapping in my belly. Then there was the other reason wedding prep had been so enjoyable – a well-built and tanned reason, standing at about six-foot-two, looking unfairly dapper in his navy suit.

'Yeah,' I said dazedly, staring up at his face. In my heels, his jaw was in my eyeline and it was a nice jaw. A hint of stubble, strong. I cleared my throat when he glanced down at me and turned my gaze back to my brother and his new wife. 'They should, everything went off without a hitch.'

'Well, they have us to thank for that,' Fletcher said with a quick wink that made me giggle. Then Rob and Tanya were upon us and I pressed a kiss to each of their cheeks as I offered my congratulations.

'Thank you, both of you, today has been amazing,' Tanya gushed, her brown skin prettily flushed against her white mermaid dress.

'Well, it's not over yet!' I gave her a quick nudge as the music for their first dance queued up and they drifted out onto the dance floor, illuminated by two spotlights. It was a lot of fanfare, but my brother always had been a little more dramatic than me.

Thankfully, one of the pros of helping to organise this wedding was that I'd got to pick my own dress. Traditionally the bridesmaid dresses went one of two ways: hideous or stunning. There was no inbetween. My dress was a light silvery colour that made my pale skin look luminous and my red hair bright and I was supremely grateful to Tanya in that moment as Fletcher turned to me and held out his hand. Couples were starting to drift onto the floor to join Rob and Tanya and Fletcher smiled at me confidently, and – yeah, I liked that. A lot.

'Shall we?' he asked, as if there were ever a world in which I'd have said no.

'I'd love to,' I said, gulping back the last of my drink and leaving the empty glass at a nearby table as I placed my hand into Fletcher's.

His hand met the small of my back and I shivered, his cologne was nice, something clean and masculine that made me want to lean closer. I had been helping Tanya practice for her first dance with Rob, and from the way Fletcher waltzed me about effortlessly, I'd guess he'd been doing the same for my brother.

We smiled when the song ended and I hesitated as I took my hand from his, only to be surprised when he gripped it a little tighter. 'Another?' he asked and I grinned. A faster, modern song came on and he began to move his hips in time, my cheeks flushed lightly and I looked away before I embarrassed myself. He tugged my hand lightly, smiling and pulling me closer until our bodies were pressed flush and my pulse jumped. I glanced quickly around, not sure how Rob would feel if he saw how cosy we were getting. The dance floor had become pretty packed though and nobody was paying us too much attention.

Fletcher's hand grazed the outside of my thigh and a shudder worked its way through me. When I looked up his blue eyes were heated and I bit my lip in indecision as I flicked another look around for any sign of Rob.

'I think I need another drink,' I sighed and Fletcher laughed.

'Sounds like a plan.'

CHAPTER ONE

SARA

This couldn't be happening. My brother's voice continued to rumble through the phone I had pressed tightly to my ear, oblivious to the maelstrom of panic now crashing through me. When I'd reluctantly agreed to go on this trip – mostly to stop Rob's whining – I'd known it was possible *he* was coming, as this was supposed to be a thank-you trip for organising the wedding. But I'd thought, *It's a big lodge, I'm sure I can avoid him for a week. Maybe he won't even come.* Ha. Apparently Rob (and whoever I'd pissed off upstairs) had other ideas. What could I say though? Um, sorry Rob, but *hell no*?

It would seem like a pretty strong reaction to someone that (as far as he knew) I'd had only a passing acquaintance with and there were a thousand reasons I didn't want to go down that rabbit hole. Firstly, it was none of Rob's business what I did or who I did it with. Secondly, he was my brother and the thought of talking to him about sex made me want to barf. Lastly… it was hard to simply tell your brother you had a one night stand with his best friend. At his wedding. And it hadn't even been worth it.

'Sara? Hel-*lo*, God I swear you are the most – Have you even been listening to anything I've said?' Rob sounded annoyed, it was a tone I was fairly familiar with as it was almost always directed at me and I'd heard my fair share of it back in September when I'd flown out to California to stay with Rob and Tanya for the wedding. Admittedly, on this occasion he was right to be mad, I had tuned out all of his words after *Fletcher will probably be on his way to pick you up by now.* That sort of seemed like information he might have wanted to mention before this whole trip was organised. The fact that I was going to have to spend several hours in the tight confines of Fletcher Harris' car and pretend like we hadn't screwed each other's brains out less than a month ago? Not that Rob knew that last part so he'd probably just thought it made 'economical sense' seeing as Fletcher apparently lived close-by.

'I'm here, I'm listening,' I said with a huff of breath, flipping my auburn bangs out of my eyes a little harder than was strictly necessary.

'So, you've packed a swimsuit then, yeah?'

'Erm–'

Rob swore colourfully, 'There's a sauna in the lodge. Bring a suit so I don't have to see your naked ass.'

'Sure,' was what I said, but internally I was screaming. Pack a *suit*? What swimwear did I even own any more? I lived in *Anchorage,* not Florida. This day was only going to get worse. I'd never even thought to ask Fletcher where he was from, I had just assumed he lived near Robert in Cali. I'd never felt more terrible about being wrong. 'Listen, I've got to go, I'll see you at the lodge, right?'

Rob murmured an affirmative and then said sternly before hanging up, 'Be nice to Fletch. He's not been himself recently.'

Not been himself? Was this me reading into things, or was Fletcher just as unhappy about my presence on this trip as I was about his? Which, honestly, seemed a little unfair – I hadn't done anything besides give him the 'best head of his life' and let's be real, there was no way it wasn't the best sex he'd ever had either. I was there. It was great. The evening up until then had been nice too, we'd laughed together and danced together and I still couldn't shake off the way his eyes had heated when I'd told him I was going to bed.

'Oh,' he sounded disappointed as he glanced away from me. 'You're tired?'

'Not at all,' I'd said with a slow smile and an answering grin had tugged at his mouth as his eyes turned molten. He wanted me and I was more than happy to oblige.

I groaned as I tried to brush the memory away, why did he have to live so close? How had I not known? Well, actually, his surfer-boy tan and blue eyes screamed California, and I had just never questioned it.

Was I even swimsuit appropriate at the moment? I frantically thought back, trying to remember my situation down there when I'd put on panties this morning – I couldn't remember anything too wild and it looked like headlights were approaching outside, so I just had to trust that I'd kept up some form of maintenance downstairs. It was a little risky because I hadn't slept with anyone since Zach, who had been a rebound fling that had fizzled almost as soon as my ass had hit his bedsheets, and I didn't always bother to shave if it was only me, myself, and I heading to orgasm-town, population... one.

I dropped my duffel to the floor and ran to my bedroom to search for some sort of swimwear before the devil himself knocked on the door. It was times like these that I was glad for the lack of stairs in my house, everything on one floor and easily accessible. It made rolling to bed after an ice cream fuelled crime documentary binge so much easier.

I rummaged around in the top drawer of my vanity, pushing aside tights that I hadn't worn in forever and a vibrator that had run out of battery, until I found the one swimsuit I owned. It was a questionable shade of black that had mostly faded to gray, at this point I supposed I just had to hope it didn't disintegrate the second I stepped into a pre-sauna shower.

Oh god, I was going to be showering. With Fletcher.

Getting sweaty in a hot sauna, *with Fletcher*. It was hard to forget someone when they kept popping up uninvited into your life. No, it was going to be fine. Fletcher didn't want to be around me anymore than I wanted to be around him, we would find an amicable way to avoid each other, take turns in the sauna and have a great (or at least not terrible) trip with minimal interaction.

How worried did I really need to be? Should I be treating this like seeing an ex for the first time? I glanced into the large mirror hanging in my hallway as I made my way towards the front door. My green eyes looked a little bigger than usual and spots of colour had flared to life at the tops of my cheekbones, this often happened when I thought about Fletcher and our night together. Which wasn't frequently, damn it.

I raised my arms and gave my pits a quick sniff, rummaged in my bag and slicked on a little extra deodorant for the inevitable nervous sweats I was going to have. Being trapped in a car with a man who was so ashamed of our night together that he'd left before I'd woken up was not going to be good for my nerves *or* my self-esteem.

I pressed my hand to my face and breathed into it just as the doorbell rang and I whipped it away so fast I almost caught myself across the cheek. He was here. Would he look the same? Maybe he wasn't as gorgeous as I remembered, all long-lashes, golden skin and floppy blonde-brown hair that I'd run my hands through while we–

No. I wasn't going there. I needed to open the door, smile and say hello, and then sit in silence for the three hours it would take to get to the cabin in the middle of nowhere that Rob and Tanya had booked.

I hadn't even had the chance to do my last minute packing checks, too distracted by anxiety and last-minute swimsuit rummaging. Well, if I hadn't already packed it the likelihood was that it was something I could live without for a week or so.

There was a blurry silhouette showing through the frosted

glass of my front door and my body trembled all over. *Don't be ridiculous,* I thought to myself, *he's just a man.*

I flung the door open and Fletcher jumped. Maybe he was just as nervous as I was trying not to be.

His cheeks were flushed from the cold and his lips parted as he took me in and well, *fuck.* He looked just as good as I remembered. He had on blue jeans, boots and a thick knit sweater and scarf. His hair looked soft, free of the gel he'd worn at Rob's wedding, and the lines by his eyes crinkled when he gave me a strained smile.

'Hi,' I said and Fletcher's smile instantly dropped like just the sound of my voice was enough to offend him.

'Hey,' he said evenly, voice empty of any emotion and the small flame of heat still burning inside me tried to gutter out, but the tightly balled fists at his side gave some idiotic part of me hope. For what, I had no clue. *He's an asshole,* I reminded myself, *don't forget about the note.* I held on to that thought, trying to keep it at the forefront of my mind as my eyes travelled over his broad shoulders and the planes of his chest, visible even through the chunky sweater. 'Are you ready?' he asked, a small bite of impatience in his voice and I nodded, lifting my duffel and moving to step out of the house but found myself blocked by a well-muscled arm. I breathed through my mouth, trying to keep the scent of his cologne out of my nose and my head as I looked up at him with raised brows.

'I think you're forgetting something,' Fletcher said, a small smirk twitching over his lips and vanishing as quickly as it came. *Hell yes,* I thought, I was trying to forget a whole damn lot – namely, *him.* He nodded behind me and I turned to look at what he was pointing at, my face burning a thousand shades of red as I saw my bikini bottoms lying on the floor by the shoe rack, apparently having fallen from my hand before I could shove them in my bag.

'Thanks,' I muttered as I bent to scoop them up and stow them away. There was something odd in Fletcher's eyes as I moved back to him, something that took me back to *that* night once more. I focused on my breathing, gesturing Fletcher to move out of the way as I stepped out of the house, locked the door and strode over to the shiny black SUV in my driveway.

Don't be stupid. He didn't want me. He'd made that abundantly clear when I'd woken up at 11AM to cold sheets and a hastily scrawled note half crumpled on his pillow. *This never happened.*

Damn right it hadn't and I was going to do my best to pretend exactly that.

CHAPTER TWO

FLETCHER

When your best friend calls you and asks if you'll pick up their baby sister and spend three hours in a car with them as a favour, you can't really say no. Especially when you went behind their back and fucked said sister. At your best friend's wedding.

I'd put up a bit of a fight, but not enough to make Rob suspicious, though right now I really wished I'd managed to find a good enough excuse to avoid this horrifically awkward encounter. It was my own fault. Not only had I slept with my best friend's sister, I'd also run away in the morning when I realised what I'd done… and just how much I wanted to do it again.

I wasn't sure how Rob would react, would he be horrified at the betrayal? Happy for any happiness I might have found with Sara? I'd been friends with him since we'd met in college as fresh-faced first years, but this wasn't a situation where I could really predict Rob's feelings. Well, it was a moot point now – there was no way she would give me another chance after I'd crept out of bed and scrawled her a note whilst still drunk.

Now I had to spend the entire car ride to Kachemak with her, likely in excruciating silence while memories of that night played on a loop in my head – as had been the case every night since the wedding. It had been a month. I hadn't been able to be with anyone else. The two dates I'd been on had felt like pulling teeth, they just *weren't her*. Not that it mattered, I'd fucked everything up before I'd been able to do even half of what I wanted to her.

Even worse than the car ride from hell, I now had to spend a week with her and her brother, acting like I hadn't made her scream my name. My dick hardened again just remembering it and I swore softly. The only way I was going to make it through this week was with my hand on my dick every night because there was no doubt in my mind that my bed would be remaining empty.

Rob had sprung Sara's invite on me, I'd already told him I would come by the time I found out that Sara would be coming too. He'd acted like it was the best thing ever and I hadn't known whether to be elated or nauseous. I would get to see her! But... I would get to see her.

Then my stomach had fallen through my ass when Rob mentioned some guy she'd been dating that hadn't ended well and so he had thought the trip might cheer her up. My hackles had immediately risen, I'd been losing sleep and she'd been sleeping her way through Anchorage? Maybe I didn't need to worry about this trip at all, maybe I was as unmemorable to her as she'd been intoxicating to me.

When she opened the door, her perfume hit my nose, just as light and fruity as I remembered. I was immediately transported back to our one night together, the way her lips had looked swollen from our kisses and the way her eyes had glazed over with lust. God, she looked good. Her heart shaped face peered up at me, green eyes pinched and her lip between her teeth as she assessed me. The next few moments were a blur, did she speak? Did I speak? I had no clue, all I could think about was how she was here in front of me, so tantalisingly close I could smell the mintiness of her breath.

I was fighting back a smirk as she picked up what looked like underwear from the floor and shoved it into her bag, but my anxiety returned as Sara walked towards my car. Now came the hard part.

She slid into the seat next to mine, her strawberry and mango scent flooding the air and making my mouth water, but I ignored her in favour of reaching for the radio and hitting shuffle on my aux. *Adele* came spilling out of the speakers and I saw her mouth twitch at my taste in music as she pulled on her belt. Even the small hint at a smile on those lips had my heart thumping hard in my chest as I pulled out of her drive. Maybe there was a chance my bed wouldn't have to be so lonely.

'Listen, about Rob's wedding–'

Sara shook her head, raising a hand and waving me off flippantly before directing her gaze out of the window. 'No, no, don't worry. It's been forgotten about. We can still enjoy the time away without any... complications.'

Oh.

'Right, yeah, of course,' was all I could think to say, disappointment a tangible taste on my tongue.

We turned out onto Ninth Avenue and began the long journey south, why had Rob and Tanya picked this place anyway? I was sure there had to be dozens of picturesque fancy lodges that weren't out beyond civilization. My best friend and his new wife were flying into Anchorage and then getting a coach out to the bay, I looked up at the rapidly greying sky and worry churned inside me. I hoped their flight would be taking off soon, before the snow had a chance to truly kick-off. Driving through the thick Alaskan flurries was not a fate I'd wish on anybody unfamiliar with them, or the roads. I'd lived here almost three years now and hadn't looked back to my life in New York. There was enough bustle in Anchorage that I didn't feel on edge but it was also a peaceful life, one I needed to combat the stress of being a relatively big-name lawyer.

I slowly began to relax as the smell of the leather seats sank into me, we'd left early to avoid traffic and the roads were relatively clear. Sara fidgeted in the seat next to me and I raised an eyebrow in her direction, spotting the goosebumps on her arms immediately and reaching for the heat.

'Thank you,' she murmured and my dick gave a happy little jump inside my pants at the sound of her voice. I needed to get my shit together.

'Anytime,' I said. God, what was with my responses today? Normally, I had no trouble with women. At the wedding, we'd got on like a house on fire – our chemistry had been off the charts and she'd made me laugh more than I could ever remember a woman doing. Yet, now it was like all the charm and charisma had dried up, alongside my balls, this past long month.

Sara flicked through a page of her e-reader without another word and I sighed quietly. I'd brought this on myself, I knew that, but being so close to something you knew you couldn't have was a form of torture I'd never experienced before.

Sara Bridges didn't want me and I wasn't sure I'd ever be good enough for her even if she did.

CHAPTER THREE

SARA

The words on the page before me were blurring and I was certain I'd missed a big plot point three chapters back. It was hard to focus with the object of several fantasies I'd recently had sitting right beside me, the warmth of his skin ghosting over me and even the scowl on his face turning me on.

It was more than ridiculous, it was shameful. This man would not be getting back into my pants ever again. He was an asshole. *An asshole who listens to Adele?*

Okay, well, assholes could still have good taste in music. It proved nothing and who knew, maybe it was a ploy to make me think he was a nice guy rather than the spawn of Satan.

There were faint dark shadows beneath his sea-blue eyes that made me wonder if he'd been having trouble sleeping. *Maybe he's been busy screwing more hapless women,* I thought snidely and then sighed. The truth was, I didn't think Fletcher was like that, he'd made me feel so comfortable I hadn't even questioned falling into bed with him straight away – it had felt utterly natural. Then to have that easy confidence ripped away had been... more than hurtful.

So why was I still staring at the cupid bow of his lips and remembering how it had felt to devour and be devoured by them?

My eyes drifted away from my page yet again and I

checked the time on my phone absently. I stifled a groan, how were we only just over an hour into this car ride? It felt like I'd been trapped in here with those big blue eyes and silky, dark cologne for a million years!

The truth was, being around Fletcher was comfortable. He had a nice smile and his deep voice was charming, relaxing me even when I didn't know I was tense. But being in this car felt so far from all of those things, there was nothing between us except heat and regret. A terrible combination.

I shifted uneasily on the leather seat and continued to ignore the looks he sent me when he thought I wasn't watching. I glanced up at the wrong moment and our eyes caught, heat travelled along my neck and up into my cheeks and I cleared my throat noisily as Adele wailed about taking it easy on her.

Fletcher's eyes were intensely focused on mine and I half-worried about the road as our stare carried on and on. Just when I thought I couldn't take it any more, he looked away and confusion rippled through me as my eyes settled on the perfectly straight line of his nose and curl of his lashes.

A sign for a gas station caught my eye through the whiteness of the small snow flurries that had started to gather speed. Fletcher opened his mouth and I *knew* that whatever came out was going to wreck me – for better or worse, I wasn't sure. So I quickly cut him off, blurting, 'Can we pull over? I need–I need to get out.'

Fletcher made the indication without a word, but a muscle in his jaw ticked and his grip on the steering wheel seemed a little tight.

I all but flew out of the car as it mostly came to a stop, rushing to the restroom even though I'd rather have died than gone inside. This one at least had a semi-dry red tiled floor and at least one cubicle had a working lock – small miracles. I stared myself down in the only non-cracked mirror stuck to the wall, this had to stop. The sex, the flirting, *it had never happened*. That's what he wanted and it was what I should have wanted too – so why did something inside me want to curl closer instead of running away?

I couldn't help thinking about the way he'd looked when we'd first met. I'd been sitting at Rob's kitchen table, looking through different nail polish colours with Tanya, when my brother had led him in and Fletcher's wide smile had snared me. I'd only met a handful of Rob's friends over the years but none of them had looked like that – not even just Fletcher's attractiveness, but the open and warm sincerity in every line of his face had taken me aback. He'd shaken my hand and then laughed bashfully at my surprise, explaining it was a lawyer-habit, and instead brought it to his lips and brushed a soft kiss along my knuckles.

You are not ruled by your emotions. Or hormones. Or whatever. I pushed the memory away and gave myself a stern nod in the mirror before exiting through the heavy door with an elbow to the handle. I debated running into the small store to grab some milk duds or something but one look at the icy set of Fletcher's face had me slowly moving back towards the car. At least I knew I wasn't the only one upset by the circumstances.

He climbed in and silently put it in reverse, manoeuvring us back out and onto the Alaskan Highway.

'Thanks,' I offered, figuring I should at least be amicable. Amicable was good. 'For stopping I mean, I–'

'I needed to get gas anyway. It's fine.'

Okaaay, maybe amicable is worse than the silence. I gave a vague nod and tried to focus back on my novel and not the man radiating heat beside me. I'd hoped a brief stop might clear the proverbial air but things seemed heavier than ever, maybe they needed an ice-breaker?

'Do you mind if I...?' I gestured to the aux and he looked at me in surprise, like he'd forgotten I was there and had just had an unpleasant reminder.

'Sure,' he said in a clipped tone. 'Wouldn't want to subject you to anything too terrible,' Fletcher muttered and I wasn't sure whether to laugh or feel indignant. We were only in this mess because of Sir Scrawls-a-lot.

I flicked through his songs, searching for the perfect tension-breaker, and had to fight back a snicker at the amount of Adele and Taylor Swift on his playlists. I finally found the right song and leaned back into my seat, trying to keep any hint of smugness from my face as the first beats of *It Wasn't Me* drifted out.

Fletcher turned to me incredulously and I burst out laughing, eventually he laughed too and the damned sound warmed me, sending tingles right down to the tips of my toes. Why couldn't I like one of the good ones?

'Nice choice,' he said, a grin pulling at his lips and capturing my attention before I remembered to look away.

'Yeah, well, it seemed appropriate,' any tension that had fallen away flooded back and Fletcher looked pained at my words, brows pulled together in concern.

'I'm sorry,' he said, 'I didn't mean for what happened between us to happen and–'

I tuned him out, staring at him incredulously as he continued to speak. He thought he needed to apologise for the sex, but not the note? I rolled my eyes and his words cut abruptly off.

'Look, we made a decision, you didn't just accidentally fall and have sex with me. We just need to acknowledge it, and move on.' I couldn't believe the words coming out of my mouth, they sounded so logical, so adult, so *absolutely the opposite* of all the things I wanted from this man.

'So,' Fletcher said, running one hand over his brow before dropping it back to the wheel, 'Rob said you'd had some sort of bad break up? Were you guys... a thing? At the wedding?'

My eyes flew wide and I spluttered at him inelegantly. Where did Rob get off shouting about my private business to every friend he had? Plus, as usual he'd come into a situation with little knowledge and thought he knew it all. I couldn't have cared less about the fling with Zach, if he thought I was upset then, well, the man sitting next to me was the culprit. But where did *Fletcher* get off asking me if I was a cheater?

'Wow. Okay, Rob doesn't know what he's talking about and I'm not that kind of person,' I said sharply and Fletcher inhaled a quick breath, as if only just realising what an ass he'd sounded like.

'Sorry, I didn't mean – Oh shit,' his gaze flew to some sort of indicator on his dashboard that I couldn't see and then to the time illuminated on his stereo.

'What's wrong?'

'I made a mistake.'

My heart galloped in response to his words, a mistake with me? 'What do you mean?'

'I think I put the wrong gas in the truck.'

For a second I could only stare at him, we were half hour away from the lodge at least and in the middle of nowhere. If we broke down, we'd be screwed until Rob and Tanya drove past. 'You did what?'

Fletcher let out a groan that had heat rising to my cheeks, 'I wasn't paying attention and I just grabbed the one I normally reach for without looking but a light just came on and now I'm suddenly wondering if I used the right stuff.'

As if on queue the engine gave a small rattle and I pressed my hands together in alarm.

'Surely not, we would have noticed it miles back if you'd used the wrong stuff.'

He shook his head and looked a little embarrassed, 'I only topped up a little so it would have had to burn through the good stuff before getting to this crap.'

'Oh God,' I breathed, so he hadn't needed gas – no, wait, *focus on what's important, Sara.* 'How did you even manage to–'

'I was distracted, okay?' The words sent a stupid thrill through me and I wiped my suddenly sweaty palms on my jeans. 'I'll continue on as far as we can without breaking my car, but then it'll be up to us.'

Great, pushing an SUV through the snow was exactly my idea of a relaxing break away.

CHAPTER FOUR

SARA

Within twenty minutes, the whine of the engine had become a deep groan and my eyes were bouncing worriedly between the deepening scowl on Fletcher's face and the snow pouring down outside. The GPS said we weren't far away now but any distance was a little too far when you've got to push a car through several feet of snow.

'Fletcher?' He gave a grunt which I took as permission to continue. 'You don't really think we need to push your car right? I mean, it's basically turning into freaking Antarctica out there. In case you hadn't noticed, I'm not exactly dressed for the weather.' In hindsight, I should have checked the forecast and prepared appropriately, it wasn't like me to be caught unawares. However, Rob *had* come along and blown a Fletcher-sized hole in all of my carefully laid plans and generally left my head spinning, so it wasn't entirely my fault that my jeans and long sleeved green cotton top were not snow appropriate. Hell, they weren't entirely Anchorage appropriate, I'd had to immediately roll the sleeves down after spending a little while outside and the cold had started sinking in. Luckily, I did have a winter coat... in the trunk of the car.

'Oh, trust me, I noticed,' Fletcher muttered and glanced uneasily outside at the rapidly white-coated scenery. I could see lights in the distance and gave a happy squeal, choosing to ignore whatever he had been implying with that comment even as it made me ache with want.

'I think that's the entrance! Tanya told me that they add lights to the road for occasions just like this. If we follow it, we should end up right outside the lodge.'

Fletcher nodded, his hands tight on the wheel as he presumably concentrated on not losing traction on the slick roads. My heart beat a little quicker as the wind picked up, rocking the car and sending a flurry of snow into us, obscuring the windscreen for a moment. 'Can you not use the wipers? Or go a little faster?'

'Right now, I don't want to get my truck to do anything except drive because it's going to give out any moment,' he snapped, clenching his jaw and I raised my hands, turning away from him to look out of the window. 'Sorry,' he said gruffly, 'I'm just trying to stay focused on getting us there in one piece.'

'Yeah well I'm pretty sure that means my head needs to stay attached to my body, so if you could not bite it off for two seconds, I'd appreciate it.' A low laugh rumbled out of him, surprising me and a faint flush built in my cheeks. That had been... rude. I was never rude. 'You bring out the worst in me,' I grumbled and he laughed again, just as the engine coughed and then guttered.

'Fuck,' he said and well, yeah. That pretty much summed it up. We were going to have to get out and push. In the snow. 'Okay, here's what we'll do. I'll get out and push, you need to steer us the rest of the way. I can see the lodge just up ahead so... try not crash my truck into it.'

I rolled my eyes but nodded. He'd clearly been talking to Rob – there was a reason I didn't drive any more. I wasn't a bad driver by any means, I just seemed to have terrible luck when it came to cars, case in point. I'd totalled three before turning twenty-five. All within a month of buying them. So, I guess Fletch's concern was slightly valid, even if it was offensive.

'Are you ready?' I called through a mouthful of snow as I stuck my head out of the window and Fletcher gave me a thumbs up. I took off the hand-brake and steered the car gently as he pushed. The car rolled forward slowly and I took a moment to be grateful that this road was flat and not on a hill, otherwise this likely would have been impossible. We rounded a small bend and there was the lodge, the roof and wooden porch covered in snow, then I saw what awaited us and I swore. I had spoken too soon.

'Fletch, we've got a problem!' I called and saw his head pop up in the car mirror. I put the brake on again and he jogged around to me, his breath fogged the air and his eyes seemed even bluer against the white backdrop.

'What is it?' he knocked errant snow from his hair and I winced as a few icy drops flicked at my face. I offered him a scowl and he grinned, making my stomach flip.

'The driveway is on a slope,' I said and his grin dropped as he swore. 'We could just leave it at the bottom?' I offered and his eyes went wide.

'You want to leave my car at the bottom of a hill to get snowed under?' His tone was indignant and I would have thought he was joking if not for the stubborn set of his jaw.

'It probably won't get snowed under–'

He was already shaking his head, 'No, come on, you know as well as I do that this is probably only going to get heavier.' I sighed and looked up at the sky, it was foggy with snowflakes and my shoulders sagged in defeat. He was right.

'So what do we do?'

'You're going to have to get out and push with me and then I'll hold it while you slip on the break again.' I nodded and slipped out of the car, grimacing at the cold. 'Here,' Fletch said, stripping off his shirt, 'I get too hot pushing the car anyway.'

He kept on his deep blue scarf and I wanted to simultaneously laugh and cry. *Who the eff does that?* Something must have shown on my face because he looked at me strangely. 'Are you okay?'

I choked, 'You–You're not– *put your shirt back on, are you crazy?'* I shrieked at him, holding the still-warm material to my chest for a second longer before flinging it back. My traitorous eyes took in his lightly muscled physique with interest, remembering how I'd traced my fingertips over the skin of his chest, my mouth went dry. I'd never seen someone so ridiculously appealing and I wanted to kick myself. How could *this* guy – the one who had just whipped off his shirt and stood standing in only jeans, boots and a scarf in the middle of a snow storm because I'd seemed cold – be the same one who'd walked out on our one wild night with only a crappy note telling me to forget all about it?

I shook my head, it didn't matter how it was possible, just that it was the truth. I didn't want to pursue something with someone who had so easily tossed me aside once before already. Even if he did strip naked in a snowstorm to keep me warm.

I moved into position next to him at the back of the SUV, sneaking a glance at him out of the corner of my eye. I'd allow myself that, I reasoned, to look but not touch if it would make it easier. His muscles bunched, his shirt had been dumped unceremoniously back into the truck and I huffed a laugh, *stubborn ass*. Though, I couldn't say I was sorry for the view as his broad shoulders tensed and he gave a grunt as he pushed that absolutely should not have turned me on but did anyway.

'Are you actually going to help? Or just ogle me shirtless in the snow?'

I jumped and brought my hands up to the bumper, digging my boots into the snow and trying not to sink. Fletcher was undoubtedly doing most of the work but I liked to think I was contributing a bit. He panted as we reached the apex of the hill, face creasing in exertion and a bead of sweat dropped from his face and rolled down his throat. I blinked and hurried to close my mouth before he could see me gaping... *again*.

The car reached the top of the drive and I breathed a sigh of relief, mostly because it meant Fletcher's shirt could now return to his body and quit distracting me.

I ran to the side and pulled up the handbrake, I could hear Fletch struggling to catch his breath as he held the car in place.

'All good,' I called and spun to run back to him and check he was alright but instead crashed into a warm chest. We went sprawling into the snow, my elbow catching him in the chin and my chest pressing firmly against his. My mouth popped open and I squeaked as I ended up across his lap and a totally different type of heat flooded my senses.

'Shit, I–'

'Sorry! I didn't mean to–'

We stopped talking over one another at the same time and the silence was somehow worse, his eyes burning into mine and his lips turning up into the small smile I both loathed and wanted to kiss. How could he still be this warm pressed into the snow with no shirt on?

'Are you part-wolf or something?' I blurted and then felt myself flush. His eyes dipped to my lips and I held my breath before pushing away, trying to ignore the way my hands dragged across his bare chest in a way that was uncomfortably familiar.

'What?' he chuffed a laugh and I offered him a hand up once I was standing and he took it, holding it a little too long to be accidental. I raised an eyebrow and he let go abruptly, reaching into the truck and pulling on his sweater.

'You're ridiculously hot.'

His head poked out of the top of his knit so quickly he got stuck, '*What?*'

I mumbled a curse under my breath, 'I mean, your temperature, in like books and stuff werewolves always run hotter than normal humans and they take their shirts off all the time because the cold doesn't bother them and–'

A hand covered my mouth and I looked up into Fletch's face in surprise. It wasn't fair really, it was beautiful here and he only looked more stunning against the snowy backdrop of fir trees and the lake off in the distance that was frozen solid. Whereas I was fairly certain my cheeks were fire engine red, my hair had started to freeze and I had just been rambling awkwardly about... werewolves? I groaned internally, it was a good thing I wasn't trying to get with Fletcher because I had zero game. Like, *zero*.

'Good to know more about what you were reading in the car. Wolf romances eh?'

'No, I – they're actually just paranormal romance,' his smirk grew and I groaned, 'let's just get inside?'

'Sure,' he said with a chuckle and playful snap of his teeth, 'I'll get the bags.'

I nodded and made my way up the stairs to the lodge, it was made of wood and absolutely stunning, towering way above my head and looking like something out of a brochure against the snow. There was a keypad in place of a key and I searched in my phone for the code as the faint sound of Fletcher digging for the bags reached me. God, I hoped Rob and Tanya got here sooner rather than later. I wasn't sure how much I trusted myself around Fletcher Harris, it had only been three or so hours since he'd picked me up and I'd already seen him shirtless. I could only pray the rest of the trip involved a lot more clothing and a lot less of Fletcher.

CHAPTER FIVE

SARA

I was dripping on the hardwood floors of the entryway by the time I made it inside, the snow melting as the central heating thawed my frozen fingers and toes. Fletcher dropped the bags inside the doorway and we took in the sprawling mass of the lodge in mutual awestruck silence.

'Were they expecting more people or something?' Fletcher said and I couldn't help but agree, it was massive for just the four of us.

'Well, I guess it's good that we have so much space, right?' *That way we can stay out of each other's way.*

Fletcher looked at me like he'd heard the thought, his posture stiffening again and his voice losing its easy rhythm when he said, 'Ah, yeah, definitely.'

The silence was thick and awkward and I scooped up my duffel from the floor without looking at him. 'Okay, well, I'm going to have a look around and find a room. See you... later?'

I glanced up and Fletcher nodded, he was facing the direction of the lounge, his jaw tight and arms crossed. I hesitated, things didn't need to be this way. But as he turned to look at me I remembered how I'd felt when I'd woken up in bed the morning after Rob's wedding. My head had been pounding with a hangover but I'd been smiling until I'd rolled over to find an empty bed and a sheet of paper that looked like it had been ripped from a hotel guide next to me. Nausea had risen up and tears had filled my eyes and standing here looking at Fletcher now, I didn't know if I could bear to see his face for another moment.

So I turned away without another word and headed up the dark wood stairs, running my hand over the bannister as I walked, and claimed one of the large bedrooms just off from the main landing. There was a cushy green armchair and small side table tucked in one corner of the balcony that overlooked the lounge and I peered over it, jumping when I found Fletcher gazing up.

I stalked off to my room with a grumble. Yes, he was hot and *yes* very briefly he'd made me feel things I hadn't ever experienced before, but all of that had been ruined the second he'd snuck out the door.

I threw my duffel down onto the bed and growled when it bounced off again, hitting the floor with a thump that had Fletcher calling up. 'I'm *fine*,' I called back and he fell silent. God, please tell me Rob would be here soon.

I pulled out my phone and grimaced, I barely had one bar of signal – this place was pretty but not well connected. Though maybe that was supposed to be part of the appeal? The tiny red notification in the corner of the screen told me I had a voicemail so I hit loudspeaker and then play as I unpacked a few things and froze a few seconds later as Rob's voice sounded out.

'Hey, I'm guessing you're on the road now and the signal might be spotty. Just wanted to let you know our flight has been delayed a little, there's apparently a snow storm coming in and we're waiting to find out if we can fly through it. I'll keep you posted, but have fun in the meanwhile and we'll see you soon.'

The message ended there and I felt my pyjamas slip out of my hands and hit the bed. Could this trip get any worse? First I had to carpool with Fletcher of all people, and then my brother's flight was delayed and now I had to spend even longer alone with him? Tears unexpectedly thickened my throat and I took a few deep breaths.

There was no need to be so dramatic, people hooked up and left early in the morning all the time, I was just one of many. I guess it hurt more because I knew Fletch, I trusted him and he had thrown that back in my face and spat on it for good measure.

A light shiver shook me as I sent Rob a quick message to say we'd arrived and then put my phone on charge. *Maybe I should try out that sauna he'd mentioned.* I was still absolutely freezing and my hair was now leaking icy water down my back, so I stripped off and tied it back, slipped on my old bikini top and bottoms and felt grateful I'd remembered to pack them even if it had been awkward for Fletch to point them out on the floor. Luckily, things were looking fairly tidy downstairs too. There was a whole row of fresh and fluffy white towels inside the mirrored, fitted wardrobe so I grabbed one and wrapped it around myself before heading back down the stairs and following a second set that took me to a basement level that smelled like water and wood.

I pulled open the heavy door to the sauna room and hung my towel on a row of hooks away from the shower – first rule of sauna etiquette, always rinse off before and after. I tipped my head up under the hot water and gave a sigh of relief. My hair plastered itself to my skull under the deluge and I felt my shoulders relax until an odd prickle on the back of my neck had my eyes flying open instinctively. It was then that I noticed the other towel hanging up and the steam curling slightly underneath the doorway to the sauna.

Fuck. Fletcher.

There was no way he hadn't seen me, if I left now it would look like I was avoiding him – which I was, of course, but he didn't need to know that. It would be rude. Plus, it's not like I could pretend I'd randomly run down here for a quick shower, in my bathing suit, when I had a perfectly nice en-suite upstairs.

Damn it. I knew what I was going to have to do now and I hated myself for it. I took one step towards the sauna and then another, sighing out a curse and then rushing forward all at once, careful not to embarrass myself further by slipping on the wet, cream-tiled floor. The door was glass and hot to the touch. I could see Fletch inside, sat on one level of the circular wooden benches with a towel wrapped around his waist.

He raised a brow as I walked into the dry heat, 'Great minds, huh. Good thing you remembered your bottoms in the end, otherwise you'd be winging it like me.'

Oh God. Was he naked? Was that what he meant? That he'd forgotten or didn't know to pack swimming trunks? I was glad I could blame the rising colour in my cheeks on the stifling temperature in the sauna but there was a gleam in his eye that told me he knew anyway.

'Yeah, good thing,' I laughed awkwardly and took a seat on one of the higher benches, letting my toes rest on the one just below. Fletcher stood abruptly and I jumped in alarm, his towel slid slightly and my heart palpitated, unsure whether I wanted it to fall completely or help him pull it up. I stayed frozen and he easily tugged the towel up like he hadn't just almost flashed me. He picked up a weirdly long spoon and plunged it into a bucket, adding more water to the heated circle stone in the middle of the room. It hissed and steam instantly billowed out, the water droplets on my skin quickly evaporated only for sweat to replace them. I licked my lips, they felt like they were burning, but the heat was nice, if a little suffocating at first. I released a long sigh and leaned back on the bench, deciding to close my eyes and pretend Fletcher wasn't there with me.

'So,' he said and I tried not to wince, there went that plan. 'What time do you think Rob and Tanya will get here?'

I opened my eyes and blinked a couple of times against the heat, my mouth felt thick, like the heat had made its way behind my lips to rub itself against my tongue. 'Oh, Rob left me a message and said that their flight has been delayed because there's a storm rolling in.'

'Oh.'

'Yeah.'

This was the worst. I wished I could be more like those people who let bygones be bygones, or better (worse?) one of those people who didn't care that they were just a quick fix and would happily do it again to pass the time. But I couldn't. I needed that connection, that *spark*, to go deeper than just physical attraction and I'd thought Fletch and I'd had that.

The heat didn't seem quite so comfortable with my maudlin thoughts bringing me down. Most women would be thrilled to have alone time with a guy like Fletcher – and in a way, I was. At least this way, we could get the bulk of our awkwardness out of the way before my brother got here. This was just… practice.

I stood slowly, not wanting to fall over as the heat started to make me a little woozy. I didn't know what it was about him, but I seemed to be ten-times as clumsy when Fletcher was around. He stood too, turning a dial near the door as we walked out to stop the heat. We moved towards the showers and I hesitated, this felt intimate even though we would have our own shower heads and would be firmly separate. The rush of cold air that hit me as we left pebbled my skin and my nipples hardened, I quickly crossed my arms over my chest and only let go to turn on the warm shower.

When I looked up Fletcher seemed amused, 'You know that's nothing I haven't seen before right? Plus, you know, it's just basic anatomy.'

'Yeah, well, that doesn't mean you get to see it again.'

The sound of the water overtook our conversation and I turned away from him in relief until he opened his stupid mouth again.

'It could mean that.' My heart stopped, surely he hadn't just said that? 'If you wanted it to.'

I turned off the water, deciding I'd finish my shower

upstairs after all. I let my anger show on my face as I walked over and wrapped myself in my towel, 'I don't know what sort of person you think I am, but I definitely have more self-respect than to let you screw me and walk out again. Need to practice your calligraphy? Or were you thinking about mixing it up this time with a balloon arch or paper mache to signal your shame?' Fletcher's face was white as I ranted but I didn't feel bad. Not at all. 'So no, I *don't* want it to happen again.'

'Okay,' he said, his voice faint and eyes wide. His lashes were wet and there was soap in his hair but I held onto my anger all the way up the stairs until I reached my ensuite and finally allowed the tears to sneak free.

CHAPTER SIX

FLETCHER

It was official – I sucked and clearly didn't know how to read a room. I was a humongous ass and Rob was going to murder me. Though, in my own defense, Sara did seem to run a little hot and cold – one minute ogling me in the snow and the next running away like all the hounds of hell were after her. But then again… I was responsible for all of that too. She didn't trust me and I couldn't blame her. The problem was, I couldn't move on and seeing her in person had only confirmed that fact. She hadn't been just a one night stand and that was what had scared me, I'd not been in a committed relationship since, well, ever. It was a lot to process, especially when the girl in question was your best friend's baby sister and therefore fucking things up with her could also mean losing Rob. *Worse,* I admitted to myself silently, *you'd lose her*. I remembered the exact moment I'd known I was in trouble, of course in hindsight it was the good kind, but still, half-drunk early-morning me had panicked.

I stretched out an arm and hit warm skin, it was smooth like silk and when I breathed in deeply Sara's fruity scent sank into me. Sara. My eyes flew open and found her sleeping naked next to me. She was on her front with the white sheets pulled up to her waist and a deep satisfaction filled me as I noticed the love-bite on her hip. Last night had been incredible. I'd never had sex like that before. I'd been with women, a fair amount in fact, but nobody had made me so intoxicated with their taste or had me begging with just a look. She'd absolutely undone me last night and I wanted more. I rolled over to check the time and groaned, 8 AM. No wonder I felt fine, I was probably still drunk and Rob would be expecting me to –

Oh God. Rob. I sat up quickly and froze when Sara mumbled something sleepily, her lips pouting adorably and nausea swept over me. What was I doing? This wasn't just Sara – it was my best friend's sister! Fuck, he was going to kill me. Sure, I'd noticed she was beautiful, but she was Rob's sister. Off-limits. A horrible thought dawned on me and as soon as it had occurred I wished I could shake it free of my mind. What if she regretted it? What if I'd just been... convenient?

I didn't want to be convenient, or the typical bridesmaid/ groomsman hookup. I wanted her and that was a problem until I could speak to her brother. If she even wanted that. Fuck, I'd gone about this completely the wrong way. I'd been having a great time last night, we'd talked and laughed and my goddamn dick had almost exploded when she pressed against me for the slow dance. What had happened? I'd planned on taking it slow. This was pretty much the opposite. Maybe... maybe we just needed to forget this whole thing. Do it over. I'd talk to Rob and I'd talk to Sara and get this whole thing sorted out. I nodded decisively and pressed a quick kiss to Sara's cheek before standing and scrawling her a quick note. I left the room, pressed the button for the elevator and sat down on the bench nearby to wait for it to arrive.

I'd woken up four hours later with a hell of a headache, a baffled Rob standing above me and Sara's room empty.

If I'd been less drunk and more rational, I would have woken her up that morning and spoken to her. Rob could have waited. Maybe everything would be different now.

But it hadn't and I still needed to have that talk with her brother. If I was going to win Sara's trust back, I needed to know that it wouldn't be in vain. I couldn't see Rob enforcing any sort of bro code really... but maybe it was better to ask for forgiveness than permission though, just in case.

I never wanted to feel like I had earlier again – to have Sara practically naked right next to me and not be able to pull her closer or feel her skin on mine. I didn't want her to be the woman I wanted but couldn't have. I wanted her to be mine, but I was going to have to earn it – for her sake and my own. I'd made a dumb choice but it was going to be the last one where Sara was concerned.

I'd dried off from the showers and headed back to my room feeling frustrated in more than one way, the image of Sara in that bikini had my pants feeling uncomfortably tight – I was just lucky the towels here were thick. Was Rob and Tanya's delayed flight a godsend? Who knew how long it was going to take them to get here, maybe I could make some progress with Sara before they arrived.

Now dry and dressed, I made my way down the stairs and examined the kitchen cupboards – compared to the rest of this place the kitchen was downright cosy. It was also empty. I looked out of the big glass windows at the back of the lodge and out at the sky, it was an ominous grey with thick white flakes beginning to fall faster than they had earlier. If this got any worse I doubted Rob and Tanya would make it here at all, which… might sort of be perfect actually. Snowed in with Sara, what could be better? I was sure we could find ways to entertain ourselves, I smirked as I pulled on my boots and the heavy winter coat I'd brought in from the car. Not that it was all about sex, of course, but it definitely didn't hurt.

If I had any hope of pulling this thing off, we were going to need food. Nobody had ever won a girl over with her stomach empty. I knew Sara had a healthy and adventurous appetite, as well as a ridiculously sweet tooth – she'd once stopped at the food court, while we'd been at the mall picking up wedding supplies, for the biggest bowl of gelato I'd ever seen, topped with enough sauce and sprinkles that I would have had a toothache. Plus, Sara was likely to curse at me enough already, let alone throwing hangriness into the mix. So a supply run was in order, even if I had to trek through a rapidly gathering snow storm for it. There was a map by the front door that showed a path to the nearest small town and supermarket, obviously only there for the holiday-makers like us, but thankfully only a twenty-minute walk away. Of course, twenty-minutes easily became forty when you were half blinded by snow and not wholly sure where you were going. The things we do for… well, not love exactly, but in this case, at least an intense *like*. Despite the chill, I grinned broadly, pulling my hood up and setting off for snacks. And booze. A lot of booze.

CHAPTER SEVEN

SARA

The sound of my phone ringing dragged me up into an upright position as I fumbled blindly for it within the covers. Rob. I groaned, I had been sulking in bed in silence, not even wanting to read, and yet *still* my brother's impeccable spidey-sense alerted him to the best time to irritate me. My annoyance momentarily faded as I considered the possibility that he was calling to say he was almost here.

'Hey! Please tell me you're on your way?'

There was a pause on the other end of the line and Rob sounded both apologetic and confused, likely because I'd never sounded more hopeful to see him in my life. 'Um, I'm guessing you haven't looked outside recently?'

'No,' I said, swinging my legs over the side of the bed and walking over to the heavy-curtained windows. I gasped as I pulled them back and saw the amount of snow outside. 'Fuck.'

'Yeah,' Rob said and lightly cleared his throat. 'Our flight was grounded. They're saying it's supposed to be one of the worst snow storms they've had in the bay for years.'

Naturally. I had the worst luck, it was genuinely unreal. 'You're still coming right?'

'Well…'

'*Rob*, you invited me to come on this holiday and you're now not planning on attending?'

'No, no,' he said quickly and I let out a breath of relief, 'we will be coming, but the storm is supposed to last for a few days, so it might be a little while until we can get a new flight out.'

I rubbed the bridge of my nose between my middle and forefinger with a groan, 'Okay well, keep me updated.'

'Ye–I–Fletch–safe–'

'What? Rob? *Hello?*' I waited a beat but all that answered me was static and I cursed as I hung up and threw the phone back on the bed. Great, no signal and snowed-in with the world's most tempting poisoned apple. Speaking of whom, I probably needed to break the news to Fletcher about Rob and Tanya – and then immediately run back up to my room and spend the rest of the trip in bed with my e-reader. Maybe I could delay that conversation for a little while.

I settled down into the plush bedding again and gave a groan of satisfaction, at least one thing was good about being here – this mattress was to die for. Ugh, I already felt old at twenty-seven. It wasn't fair. The bed was way too big for one person though and I star-fished in it for a second before my thoughts took me back to the one person available to adequately fill it. *Not happening*.

I curled on my side and tried to read but when ten minutes had passed and I hadn't taken in anything I'd read, I sat up abruptly. *What if Fletch doesn't know about the big storm?* Surely my outburst in the shower rooms hadn't scared him off that badly, but what if it had and he was now out there stranded in his stupid shiny SUV being swallowed by the snow?

No, the car doesn't work. I let out a breath of relief, he definitely hadn't driven anywhere then and I was pretty sure Uber wouldn't be picking up right now, even if we did have signal. But what if he'd gone for a walk, to *get some air* or *clear his head* as guys were so often fond of doing?

I cursed my brain and rolled begrudgingly off of the bed, pulling on some extra thick, comfy socks and poking my head out of my bedroom door. 'Fletch?'

Nobody replied and I wondered if he was mad and ignoring me.

'Fletcher? Rob called.'

Still nothing.

Starting to feel a little worried now, I walked down the stairs, thinking maybe he was in the sauna again or one of the downstairs bedrooms and couldn't hear me. Both were empty and I was out of breath by the time I ran back up the stairs to the ground floor and scanned the lounge. My eyes snagged on the coat hook and fear spiked through me, where was his coat? His boots? Oh God, Rob had told me to be nice to him, what if he had left and I had to break the news to my brother that his friend had gone out in a snowstorm and become an icicle? Plus, yes, I was mad at Fletcher but I didn't want him to be hurt.

He's fine, he's probably just... on the balcony!

I ran to the back of the lounge and looked out of the floor to ceiling windows that led out to a balcony. Nothing. *Shit*. Where was he? If he wound up hurt just because I'd yelled at him...

I hurried over to the front door and tugged on my coat and boots. I peeked out of the long window next to me and grimaced. There was snow as far as the eye could see. It swirled through the air with an increasingly audible moan, the sky thick with white flakes. Fletcher's car sat safe underneath a ledge and I wanted to laugh as I realised he had been right, if we'd left it uncovered at the bottom of the drive it definitely would have been snowed-under. I took a deep breath and jumped on the spot slightly before flinging open the door and falling short as I was about to plunge outside.

'Where the hell have you *been*? I've been looking all over for you!'

Fletcher stood on the other side of the door, only his eyes were visible above the scarf he'd tugged up and over his mouth and nose, and they were comically round as they looked at me. 'You have?'

'Yes! Rob called, their flight has been grounded because of, well, all that,' I said, gesturing behind him and Fletcher nodded, an odd gleam in his eye that made me step back suspiciously. What was he up to? He gave a light shiver and I retreated further into the entryway to let him in, he closed the door behind him and immediately shucked off his boots with a low groan.

'Are you okay?'

He panted a laugh as he unwound his scarf from his face and a swooping sensation started in my stomach as I saw his sweetly pinkened cheeks. 'Yeah, I will be as soon as I can get the snow out of my socks. My feet are freezing.'

I stifled a giggle, not wanting to laugh with him when I was still mad – near-death by popsicle incident aside.

'What were you doing out there?'

Fletcher gave a light shrug, as if being out in the middle of a snow storm was no big deal. 'I had a feeling there was a storm coming in and we didn't have any supplies, there's a supermarket about a twenty-minute walk away so I headed out.'

I stared at him, 'You must have been gone for longer than an hour though.'

The pink in his cheeks deepened and I couldn't pull my eyes away, 'Yeah, I, um, got lost.'

'You're such an idiot, Fletch.'

'Well, I didn't want hunger to give you an excuse to be grumpy with me,' he said with a roll of his shoulders after peeling off his coat.

'I don't think I really need any more excuses, do you?'

We fell silent until my stomach grumbled loudly and he laughed. 'Good thing I went out and got us some food, otherwise you'd be forced to eat me.'

Don't blush. Don't blush. Don't blush. The tell-tale sting of my cheeks horrified me as I remembered consuming him *veeeery* slowly the last time I'd seen him. Fletch coughed to cover a laugh but mostly ignored my reaction as he carried bags towards the kitchen.

'What do you want?' he called behind him and I froze between steps as I followed him into the small kitchen. 'For dinner,' he amended as he stuck his head out of the doorway to look back at me and then rolled his eyes. I couldn't help but read into every single thing he was saying – why was he not as freaked out as me that we were stuck in here together for at least the next few days with nothing but each other, the past, and our libidos for company? 'Okay, well, I'm thinking soup because I'm not really sure how to use this oven or anything yet.'

'Sounds good,' I croaked and sat down at the dining table big enough for ten, it ran the length of the back wall in front of the floor-to-ceiling windows, at least we wouldn't have to sit next to each other.

Fletcher emerged from the kitchen a few minutes later with two bowls and spoons in his hands, setting them down on the table before plopping himself down next to me. *So much for separation*, I sighed.

'I hope tomato is okay, they didn't have a huge selection and I wasn't sure what you liked.'

It was disconcerting that he cared enough about me to think about soup that hard, what was his angle?

'Tomato is good, thanks.' It was quiet for a moment as we ate in silence, I kept my eyes on the room in front of us, trying to ignore the demanding presence right next to me. It was very pleasant in here really, there was a large white mantelpiece above the fireplace which was already stacked with logs. The sofas were large and plush in a sweet cream colour that was soothing against all the dark wood in the room –

'Are you going to ignore me forever?' Fletcher asked, his voice a little quieter than usual, and I chanced a look at him to find his eyes on his soup and a frown tugging at his bottom lip.

'I just don't understand you,' I said honestly. 'We sleep together and you leave the next morning, telling me to forget it ever happened via a *note*, but suddenly you care enough to want to know what sort of soup I like? I don't buy it. If you're just trying to sleep with me again–'

He cut me off with a sigh, running his hand across his face before looking up at me with a stark expression, 'I never meant to leave.'

I choked on a laugh, what did that even mean? How could you accidentally write a note and walk out the door? His eyes roved over my face, his jaw tightening at whatever he saw on it.

'What I mean is, I was always going to come back.'

I stared at him, not sure if he meant what he was saying or just trying to ease the tension seeing as we were now stuck together for the next few days.

He continued on when I said nothing, 'I was still drunk when I left, I barely remember scrawling you that note and I definitely didn't mean it how you took it – or how I wrote it, I guess.'

'Why leave at all?' I finally managed through my dry mouth.

'I needed to talk to Rob. I'd gone behind his back and–' Fletcher glanced at my mouth and then away, clearing his throat, 'I needed to do it all the right way. I had no intention of coming to your room that night but, well, you're very charming when you want to be.'

I wasn't sure I believed him, but God, *I wanted to* – and that was what made it worse. Even if what he said was true, how could I trust that he wasn't going to leave again as soon as our stint in this snowy-prison was done? My head was spinning with his words and I pushed away from the table with a quarter of my soup still left in my bowl.

'I-I need to think about... things. I'll see you in the morning, all right?'

'Sara–'

I shook my head and made my way up the stairs to my

room. I had a feeling I was going to have a very sleepless night ahead of me.

CHAPTER EIGHT

SARA

I'd hoped that with yesterday's early start I would drop off to sleep quickly, instead I laid in bed staring at the ceiling in the dark with Fletcher's words swimming around in my head. Every time I would get close to dropping off my thoughts, unbidden, would turn to the way Fletcher's hands would feel on my body. The remembered heat of his mouth on my skin, and my eyes would fly open as I took my frustration out on the mattress, beating my fists down on either side of me until I was ready to attempt sleep... only to repeat the process. My phone had read 5AM by the time I'd finally succumbed to exhaustion, my mind sinking gratefully into nothingness. Until now.

I'd slept most of the afternoon away, getting up only to open the curtains slightly to let in some natural light and a view of the snow. It was sunny but I could hear the high winds creaking the lodge and the one leg I periodically stuck out of the duvet quickly chilled from the cold air.

I'd been reading for the last hour or so when my e-reader beeped at me again and the screen went dark. I guessed that meant it was officially time for me to get up and face the music. Or... I thought back to the gorgeous main bathroom on this level and the huge bath in it that I had spotted while exploring yesterday. *Wow*, had it really only been twenty-four hours ago?

I grabbed a fresh bath towel from the cupboard and my bag of toiletries and poked my head out of my door cautiously. All was quiet and I breathed a quiet breath of relief as I made my way to the bathroom and turned on the taps for the bath. It had three, because it was almost the size of a small pool. Like, seriously, I could have done laps.

Once it was obscenely full of water and bubbles, I cautiously dipped a toe in and hissed in delight at the scalding temperature. I stepped down two steps and sank in, a little nervous about my additional weight making the bath overflow, but the excess water started to drain away easily and I felt my muscles finally relax as the heat sunk in. Alaska was beautiful in a distantly cold way a lot of the time, but it was at a time like this when, soaking in a giant, hot bath, I recalled all of the positives that came with living so far away from the rest of my family. Rob still lived near my mom in California, our dad had passed when I was nine and he was fourteen, but I had opted to move away, needing a change of pace and scenery. Luckily, my job was pretty flexible and I could do everything from home. Rob was a doctor and didn't have the same luxury – frankly I was shocked he was able to have time off for his honeymoon and then this holiday almost back-to-back, the perks of running your own practice I guessed.

I had definite bathroom envy right now, this whole room sparkled. It was wall-to-floor marble with a walk-in wet-room style shower with a ginormous shower head. The bath took up the left wall and was set deeply into the marble floor where a ledge and long frosted window ran, I waded over and rested my hands on the ledge with my face atop them. I would have to face Fletcher at some point and I didn't know what I was going to say. What was he expecting me to say? I loosed a long breath and unhooked the window, pushing it open just enough for me to peer outside at the snow as I wallowed. The sun had started to set and a chill ran across my bubbly forearm, I shivered, but not because of the cold. I had a decision to make and I didn't know whether to trust my head or my heart.

What Fletcher had said... made sense. I mean, it was dumb as fuck, but it had hurt so much when I'd woken up alone because it had shocked me, he didn't seem like that kind of guy. We'd gotten to know each other fairly well during wedding prep, otherwise I never would have slept with him. I wasn't a one-night-stand kind of gal – Zach notwithstanding as that had been a desperate rebound and had left me feeling gross. I honestly didn't believe Fletcher had a malicious bone in his body and his explanation definitely helped – but it didn't erase the past, or the hurt that came along with it.

I pushed away from the ledge and let myself sink under the water, slicking my long hair back and away from my face as I came up again. I supposed it was more than just my head and heart, there were also my body and hormones to contend with – both of which seemed to have Fletch's name branded across them like slutty cheerleaders screaming for his attention. Begging for it, for him.

My head said logically, he could be making this shit up. Maybe he wanted to get back in my pants again – which admittedly, was a little big-headed of me – or maybe he just wanted to ease the tension between us for the few days we'd have to spend alone together. It's possible I was up here obsessing over absolutely nothing and Fletcher was expecting us to continue with the conversation he'd raised yesterday. But if I listened to my gut, my heart, I knew he was a good guy – sometimes to the point of ridiculousness like whipping off his shirt in the snow for me, or wading out into a snowstorm to get me soup. My brain got caught up on that image of him surrounded by white snow, deep blue scarf fluttering in the wind and showing off tantalising glimpses of his chest and the dark hair that trailed across his pecs and down the hard line of his stomach disappearing down to–

I cut the thought off. It was the hormones. Zach had been... average in bed. My aim had been to go out, have fun and forget Fletcher. If anything, the date had done the opposite as I waited for the spark Fletch and I'd had to appear, waiting for the kiss to turn electric and for my pleasure to build until–

Crap. If I didn't get it together, there was going to be a very slim chance of me making it through this trip without making *out* with the he-devil himself.

What was the worst that could happen? *Um, you sleep together, it's just as good as you remembered and you're officially ruined for all other men?* I scoffed and then grimaced, I wouldn't tell him so because his ego was liable to inflate, but Fletch was undeniably excellent in bed.

You trust him. You let him in. He breaks your heart. Well, he'd have to have my heart in the first place for that to happen. I palmed some water and let it run across my skin while I considered. It was likely though, I wasn't good at one-time things, Zach had only been my second and I was still paying for my first. So if I did this, if I decided to trust that what he'd said was true and he'd never meant to leave, then I had to go in knowing I might get my heart broken. Though I supposed it was a risk everyone took with any relationship. *Rob would probably kick Fletch's ass though* and that thought gave me a little comfort mostly because it was so ridiculous. My brother was very much more of a lover than a fighter.

My fingers and toes were starting to prune and I knew I needed to get out soon before the water became cold and ruined the relaxation. I was probably over-thinking all of this anyway. Fletch and I had slept together once, just over a month ago now, it seemed pretty unlikely that he still wanted to pursue something. I had no doubt that a lot of women were probably chasing him.

I pressed down on the plug and the water started trickling away with a soothing *shush*. I stood up slowly, hooking the window closed again and then climbed up the steps to the edge of the bath. My toes had just sunk into the deep, soft cosiness of the bath mat when the room was plunged into darkness.

CHAPTER NINE

SARA

I froze, blinking in the sudden dark. The water on my body was rapidly cooling and I shivered as I reached half-blindly for where my towel hung on the heated rack. I could see only by the glow of the snow outside coming in from the large window and once the bath water had finished draining and silence overtook the room, all I could hear was the howl of the wind. It seemed that the snowstorm was finally out in full-force.

The silence sank into me and I stood still for a moment as I waited. Normally these places had back-up generators that would automatically kick-in during a power outage, but after another five minutes passed and I stood dripping onto the floor I decided that if there were generators here, they weren't coming on.

The lodge looked different in the dark, chairs and tables making unfamiliar shapes that had my heart leaping into my throat as I walked back to my room to get dressed. The wind made the lodge creak and I jumped, spinning around as I reached my door to check the space behind me. Empty. *Duh. What were you expecting? A serial killer?* God, I needed to watch less of those documentaries.

I slipped inside my room and immediately stopped, breath held as I tried not to make a sound. There was someone standing in my room. Too tall to be Fletcher, an arm moved and I cried out, running backwards and tripping over my feet. I lost hold of my towel at some point in the tangle of my own legs and then Fletch was there.

'Sara? Are you okay?' He pulled me to my feet and I clung to him with my arms around his neck. He inhaled sharply, 'You're wet.'

'I–My towel fell–'

He quickly stooped to pick up with me still attached to his side like a limpet, spotting the bright white on the wooden floors easily and wrapping me in it securely. Maybe later I would feel embarrassed to have been found sprawled naked on the floor in front of Fletcher, but right now I had bigger problems – someone was in our lodge.

Fletcher opened his mouth but I pressed my hand over it, my pulse beating a frantic rhythm as I lowered it again and whispered, 'There's someone in my room. Do you think they cut the power?'

It was too dark for me to make out the expression on Fletch's face but I felt his muscles tense underneath his shirt as he grasped my hands and pulled me away from him. His steps were silent as he moved towards my door and peeked around the edge of the door frame while I stayed out of sight around the corner. Fletcher rushed into the room and I gasped. Then his laughter reached me, billowing out so fiercely that I felt heat instinctively rise in me as I ran over to him.

'What is it?'

'Oh, nothing, you're just possibly the most adorable person I've ever met,' he said and then mimicked me in a high falsetto, *'Do you think they cut the power?'* before breaking out into laughter again.

I moved closer and cursed when I realised why he was laughing so hard, I couldn't help but join in. A robe was clasped in his fist by the hood, ripped off of the hooks in the corner where it had hung.

'Wow, okay. I'm an idiot, let's agree to never tell anyone about this? Deal?'

Fletcher was laughing too hard to answer me, wiping tears from his eyes as he bent double and that same stirring filled me. Suddenly I was very, very aware of my own nakedness and his proximity. His laughter died away as if he too had just had the same thought and I coughed lightly in the silence.

'Well, um, thanks for the 'rescue' I guess,' I said and Fletcher chuckled once more, the sound reverberating deeply and setting the hair on my arms on end.

'My pleasure,' he said and I knew if I could see him right now he would likely be smirking. 'Why don't you get dressed and come downstairs? I've found some candles so I'll be able to keep an eye out for any other sleepwear trying to 'break in'.'

I laughed and rolled my eyes, 'I'm never going to live this down am I?'

'Probably not,' he agreed.

'Luckily I have a few persuasive tricks up my sleeve to help you forget.' The words were out of my damn mouth before I could think them through, his surprise was almost tangible in the air between us and I could hear the smile in his voice when he replied.

'I look forward to it.'

The room felt colder as soon as Fletcher left and I hurried to drop my towel and pull on the complimentary robe before digging around in my duffel for some underwear and socks.

Oh God.

My hands dug deeper into the bag as I rummaged, trying not to panic. I pulled out a pair of thick socks and tried to cast my mind back – had I actually packed any panties? I'd been so concerned about the swimsuit that I wasn't sure I'd remembered to bring any. I stared down at the shadowy form of my bag in horror. Had I self-sabotaged or was this a sign? First I got snowed-in with the guy I was trying *not* to sleep with and then I discovered I didn't pack any underwear? Like, none at all? Maybe once it was daylight I'd be able to find them in the bag.

The dark was starting to creep me out again so I hurried into a pair of soft and comfy PJ pants and an oversized tee before tying up my mostly dried hair into a messy bun. There. Easy, scruffy, clearly not seductive. *Except for the fact that you're currently commando.*

Sara emerged from upstairs a few minutes later, her hair was still slightly damp and the red strands curled towards her temple in sweet ringlets that I wanted to tug. She'd found a blanket from somewhere and had it draped around her shoulders as she sat down near me on the couch, peering shyly upwards and darting her eyes away quickly.

'I take it you made it down the stairs without any further attacks?' I teased and she turned a light shade of pink that only made her more alluring in the candlelight.

'Yes, thank you,' she gave a small, embarrassed laugh. 'Do me a favour and don't tell Rob. He'll only try and bring it up at the most awkward moments to embarrass me.'

I grinned at her and felt a curl of anticipation at the way the colour in her cheeks deepened and her gaze fell to my mouth. I licked my lips slowly, deliberately and her head jerked up as she looked around the room. I let out a low laugh, 'I make no promises and favours won't come cheap. I've already rescued you once tonight.'

She raised a cocky eyebrow, 'From a robe.'

'Yes, well, *you* didn't know that at the time, now, did you?'

'True,' she laughed lightly and something inside me relaxed at the sound. I hadn't been sure if saying what I had last night would do more harm than good, but things between us definitely seemed... better. 'When do you think the power will be back on? I was surprised the generators didn't automatically kick-in.'

I shrugged, 'I've not been in a snowstorm before so I don't know how the generators work, but a fancy place like this must have them, especially out in the middle of nowhere. This AirBnB is wild, I don't know how Rob and Tanya found this place.'

'It's just like Rob to pick something obscure, force me to come and then not show up himself.'

I raised an eyebrow, 'Pretty sure he didn't schedule the snowstorm, sweetheart.'

'He would have if he thought it would annoy me.'

I laughed loudly, 'Times like this I'm glad I'm an only child. Anyway, I'll go down to the basement level tomorrow when there's daylight again and take a look, I'm sure we can just flip a switch or something and they'll turn on.'

'And if they don't?'

She looked worried, one lip pulled in between her teeth. I couldn't resist. I leaned in and brushed that bottom lip with my thumb, exhaling roughly as she let it go for me to stroke the full length. 'They will, but even so, we have candles and food – I didn't really buy anything perishable aside from milk, which I'm pretty sure we can put outside to keep cold.' I grinned at her and her mouth popped closed as she gave a light nod. 'so what do you want to do tonight?' The question felt loaded and I could tell from her big pupils that she agreed. I wanted to know where her thoughts had gone but before I could say anything she sat up straighter, pushing down whatever it was she was feeling.

'How about a movie?'

'...The power's out.'

'My laptop is charged and I had a couple things downloaded.'

I considered it, movie in the dark, snuggled up to Sara... 'Okay, sounds good.'

She leaped off the couch and hurried up the stairs to grab

the laptop and I took a few moments to settle myself. We were going to take this slow, the way we should have done originally. I liked her too much to want to mess this up again. I readjusted myself in my pants and built up the fire in the fireplace a little more as I waited for her to get back with the movie.

Sara padded down the stairs and then hesitated looking at me, 'Where should I put it?' I wanted to groan, was everything out of this woman's mouth a euphemism?

'I'll bring over one of the chairs and we can put it in front of us.' I moved the chair over and could feel Sara's eyes on my back as I placed the laptop on it and then settled back onto the couch with her.

'So what movies have you got?'

She blushed a little, 'Erm, *Love, Actually* and...'

I raised an eyebrow, 'And?'

'Indiana Jones. The first one.'

I gave a startled laugh, 'Those are absolute polar opposites.'

'I wasn't sure what mood I'd be in!' She said defensively and I laughed again, hitting play on *Love, Actually* and then wished I'd picked something else when Martin Freeman and Joanna Page came onto screen awkwardly fucking. We both studiously looked only at the screen but my attention quickly wandered as I breathed in Sara's fruity smell and felt the warmth from her hand close to mine. My eyes found hers and her lips parted, caught on an exhale that I wanted to feel on my mouth as she moaned.

I leaned a little closer, just a fraction of an inch, enough to feel it when her breathing hitched and see it when her thighs pressed together. She wanted me.

Sara pushed up and out of her seat, closing the laptop lid abruptly and I raised an eyebrow at her.

'Let's... do something else,' she suggested and I grinned, liking where her head was at. Until she picked up a pack of cards I'd left lying on the side, I'd found them discarded in a drawer in the kitchen and hadn't put them back yet.

She wanted me. But she didn't quite trust me. Not yet.

CHAPTER TEN

SARA

'I fold,' I groaned, tossing down another hand of cards onto the floor between us. It felt safer, having this space between our bodies and something to focus on. My thoughts had been able to roam free sitting on the couch and watching that movie and not only did they run free, they ran *dirty*. It wasn't helpful, I'd decided to take things slow with Fletcher. I liked him and wanted to make sure he liked me, rather than being driven by this heat between us.

I took a swig of the tequila bottle we had between us and sighed, I'd lost and that was our forfeit. When Fletch had brought it out I'd raised my eyebrows and asked if that was a good idea, especially on an empty stomach. He'd grinned and brought out cheese and crackers, unrepentant, and in the end I'd laughed and waved it over. I was in control, regardless of the alcohol.

'Seriously, is this like a trick pack of cards or are you cheating? I don't get how you keep winning.'

Fletcher grinned, 'I'm not good, you're just that bad.'

'Personally I just think you're trying to get me drunk and we both know *that's* a terrible idea.' *Open mouth, insert foot.* Why did I get so loose-lipped when I drank anyway? Fletch had only had two shots max and one was basically voluntary.

His smile dimmed slightly, 'I don't think it would be as

bad as you think, but rest assured,' Fletcher crawled closer, trampling the cards on the floor between us and taking my chin in his hand, 'the next time I fuck you, you're going to be stone-cold sober. And you're going to enjoy it just as much as me.'

My cheeks flushed red but I didn't look away, alcohol apparently made me bold, too. Not that I was especially shy, but I also wasn't hugely forward either. He leaned back with an entirely satisfied look on his face, like I'd given him exactly the reaction he'd wanted. We played another hand of poker and this time Fletcher lost. I watched the movement of his golden throat with fascination as he swallowed the tequila. He offered me the bottle and I took it with a small sip that burned almost as hot as I did.

I leaned forwards to grab my cards, scooping them into my palms and then gasping as my hand collided with something cold and solid. I lurched towards the tipping tequila bottle in panic and Fletch caught me with one arm as he moved closer, snagging the bottle with the other hand. He had the tiniest freckles dotted across his face, I smiled, they were like small secrets, luring me in like they were about to whisper. I leaned in a little closer and Fletch's eyes were on my face, his breath smelling like tequila, but his eyes were still sharp, like mine. He leaned in a fraction closer and my heart began to race – had I imagined that? Or did he want to kiss me as much as I wanted to kiss him?

The tequila bottle thunked safely to the floor but I barely heard it, too focused on the soft breathing of the man in front of me and the way it caught when I moved slightly closer. I wasn't sure who breached the last of the space first, but suddenly we were kissing. Fletch's mouth was hard on mine, unrelenting like he'd packed all his want and frustration into that one kiss, and I panted into it. It was so much better than my hazy memories of the night of the wedding could have prepared me for, the demanding softness of his lips, the tempting stroke of his tongue.

I pulled back to trail a kiss down his jaw, smiling at his groan, 'I thought you said I'd be sober?'

Fletcher watched me in amusement, his lips tipping up as he moved away, 'You will. This is just... a kiss. Trust me, when we're about to have sex, you'll know it.'

'So cocky,' I said with a roll of my eyes, ignoring the disappointment flaring through me as I moved slightly further away from him.

We continued to pass the tequila between us for a few more minutes in silence, his eyes like a live wire on my skin.

'Let's play a game,' Fletch said and I laughed because he sounded like that guy from the horror movie.

'What game do you want to play?' I asked with a bite to my lip and Fletch grinned, leaning forward and tugging on it playfully.

'Stop that, it's distracting.'

Fire burned in my veins at his words, I liked the way his eyes lingered on my hair, my eyes, like he was trying to visually consume me to remember this moment.

'Let's play Truth or Dare,' he said eventually and waved me off when I scoffed. 'I want to get to know you better and what better way to do it than with tequila, poker and a game for high schoolers?'

I grinned, 'Okay, fine, what are the rules?'

Fletch's answering smile was big and a riot of butterflies made my palms a little sweaty as I reached for the bottle. 'You pick either Truth or Dare before you view your cards, whoever loses the hand has to do either the Truth or Dare – but you can't pick one or the other more than twice in a row.'

'Sounds fun,' I clapped my hands together excitedly and then pointed at the cards. 'Gimme.'

Fletcher dealt the cards and then called out, 'Dare.'

I laughed, of course he would pick dare. He just wanted to kiss me again. 'Truth.'

I set my cards down confidently, my smile fading as I saw his three of a kind beating my doubles. 'Shit.'

Fletch looked wicked as he tipped back the tequila and caught a droplet of it on his tongue. I was absolutely riveted but his words made me groan. 'Tell me what happened with your boyfriend – Zach?'

'Okay, firstly, *not my boyfriend*. Rebound sex. Very mediocre. Truly nothing to tell.'

Fletch's brow wrinkled, 'Rob seemed to think you were heartbroken – in fact, that was pretty much his exact wording.'

I shrugged, 'Rob doesn't know what he's talking about. I only told him about Zach because I was sad about–' I cleared my throat and looked away, wishing I could unsee the way his face fell at my words. 'So, yeah. Zach was an experiment, I had one hookup with him and that was pretty much it. We met in a bar, got drunk, hooked up and that was it. We tried to go on a date or two but it just… wasn't the same.'

'Same as with me?'

I looked at him shrewdly, 'That's more than one question, bucko.' Thing was, it was true. Zach just didn't compare to the night I'd spent with Fletch, there'd been no heat, we'd barely had enough of a connection to be friends let alone anything more.

Fletcher stood with the tequila in his hand, finishing the last bit in one gulp before going off to presumably grab more. My eyes dropped to his ass as he reached up and into a top cupboard in the kitchen, his cosy PJ bottoms hugging every part of him, he cleared his throat and my eyes leapt up to find smug humour written across his face. He waggled his eyebrows and I laughed shyly as he made his way back over to me.

'If you'd been listening instead of ogling me, you would have had the opportunity to pick our drink. But you weren't, and now you're stuck with vodka.'

'Do we not have any mixers?' I whined and he sighed playfully, tweaking my nose as he leaned forward to collect the cards again.

'I could only carry so much back from the store in the middle of a snowstorm, Sara.'

I grinned, 'Okay, fair enough. I guess your motivations weren't totally nefarious.'

'Well, I didn't say that,' Fletch chuckled as he dealt out the next lot of cards.

'Dare,' I declared boldly, internally wincing, but I couldn't pick Truth forever. Fletcher picked Dare too and there was a challenge in his gaze that made me sit straighter as I looked over my cards.

'Ready?' He asked and I nodded, 'Okay, three, two, one–' Fletcher groaned and I laughed as he saw my cards. 'Full house,' he sighed, 'what's my dare then, gorgeous?'

I took a sip of vodka as I considered him, and then another. There was a bright eagerness to his face that made my heart sing, he looked like he would take anything I dished out and still beg for more.

An idea began to form and I smiled slowly, 'I dare you... to take off all your clothes – no! To strip for me... and then run into the snow.'

Fletcher gaped, blinking at me before laughing and I joined in, relieved, worried for a second that I'd gone too far. He stood and anticipation was a live thing, coiling inside me and driving my adrenaline up as he lifted off his gray tee slowly, stretching upwards as I let my gaze roam down. I half-wished the power wasn't out so I could play some music, maybe something like *Leave Your Hat On.* My eyes glazed over as he toyed with the waistband of the pyjama bottoms, tugging it down to expose one hipbone before pulling it back up and showing the other. Fletcher abruptly tugged them down and I stifled a gasp at the sight of the large lump in the front of his black boxers. A surge of satisfaction mounted knowing I wasn't the only one aching and hot and bothered right now. He whipped the boxers down and off and was running towards the door before I'd got more than a glimpse of him, a laugh startled out of me at his yell as the cold air hit him.

I was cackling wildly as I rushed to my feet, swaying only a little as I staggered to the door just in time to see his bare ass meet ice as the wind bowled him over. I ran out into the snow and helped him up with a grin that he met with his own. Snowflakes were caught in his hair and eyelashes and his teeth kept chattering but we were laughing as I wrapped his arm around my waist for warmth and pulled him back to the lodge.

CHAPTER ELEVEN

FLETCHER

Sara bundled me in front of the fireplace in what felt like a million blankets as soon as I got my underwear back on. She hadn't stopped smiling since we'd come inside and my own face was starting to ache too. There was a strange sort of exhilaration at seeing her so clearly happy and knowing I'd been the cause. My shivers subsided fairly quickly, especially with the aid of the vodka. The expression on her face as I'd stripped for her was going to be burned into my memory forever and was currently doing a pretty good job of heating me too. She'd looked at me like she was starving and I was quickly becoming familiar with the sensation as I ran my eyes over her. But I'd meant what I'd said – I didn't want to rush this and I didn't want her to have alcohol as an excuse for falling into bed with me. I wanted her to want me and I wanted her to know it too.

I was soon sweating beneath the pile of blankets but I didn't dare move because Sara was pressed to my side, warm and smiling and her hair looked like flames in the light of the fire. I wasn't sure what Rob's game was, but I believed Sara when she said nothing much had happened between her and Zach.

'If it helps,' I said hesitantly, not really sure whether being this vulnerable was going to be good or bad for us, 'I haven't been with anyone since you. It wasn't the same.'

She smiled as I repeated her earlier words and a spiral of relief swept through me, she meant more to me than a casual hookup and I needed her to know that, to have all the facts before she wrote me off completely. Her green eyes seemed brighter than usual as they met mine and a little dart of pain flitted through my heart – she was so beautiful.

'Sara,' I said quietly and she turned to look at me, hesitation still showing on her face in the tilt of her brows and slight scrunch of her nose. 'Truth or Dare?'

There was a pause as she considered, running her eyes over me as if searching for an answer to a question bigger than the one I'd asked. 'Dare,' she said eventually and my breath shook as I released it. Did she want me? My palms were slick from more than the heat as I shrugged off a couple of layers and turned to face her. Was she ready to make a choice yet? Had she seen in my face what I was going to ask her before I said it?

'I dare you,' I whispered, 'to kiss me.'

A riot of emotions crossed her face, lust making her bite her lip, desire deepening the green of her eyes and dilating her pupils, anticipation quickening her breaths. She leaned in and longing tore through me like lightning, ravaging and burning and melting me before her lips even met mine.

They were soft and light, a ghost of a kiss and I held perfectly still until she started to pull away. 'That was barely a kiss,' I murmured, sinking my hand into her hair, 'kiss me like you mean it.'

Sara's gasp had my dick bobbing a greeting, if she pressed any harder against me she was definitely going to understand just how much she affected me – though I supposed it was a bit of a moot point after my strip show.

Her mouth covered mine fiercely, nipping at my bottom lip and sending her tongue darting over mine in a tease that had thoughts spinning through my head – having her in my lap riding me, spread against the table, pressed against the wall... I pulled back before I could lose control completely and kissed her forehead gently. 'You're incredible.' She blushed a little and I pressed a kiss to each of her cheeks too. 'Don't ever forget it.'

My head hurt. Fletcher and I had consumed an ungodly amount of alcohol last night and yet... I'd woken up in my own bed, thankfully. Fletch had walked up the stairs with me, eventually swinging me up into his arms because I'd been taking so long, and deposited me on the floor outside of my bedroom with a simple *Goodnight*, before walking off to his own room on the other side of the main bathroom.

Several things played on a loop in my mind though, the kisses for one – they had been everything I'd been fantasising about for the last few weeks. Fierce but gentle, dirty but soft. The other thing that had occupied my thoughts – okay, fantasies – as I climbed out of bed and peered cautiously outside, was Fletcher taking off his clothes. I'd never had a strip tease before and I had enjoyed it. A lot. Had already thought about it a few times this morning, having woken up so turned on I had already been wet when my hands had finally drifted down below my waistband.

The snow continued to pour down outside but the wind had at least seemed to have eased off a bit. I chanced a quick wash in the ensuite bathroom, the water was barely warm and I knew that first on the agenda today had to be fixing the fuse box. It was likely a good thing that there wasn't much hot water though, taking my clothes off for any reason seemed far too tempting right now with Fletcher just down the hall and the memory of his kisses still burning through me.

With the bright whiteness of the snow outside illuminating my room, I emptied my entire duffel bag on the bed and groaned. I definitely hadn't packed any panties. *Commando it is*, I sighed and then tugged open my bedroom door after quickly pulling on my thickest pair of blue joggers and a comfy tee. Fletch was sitting in the armchair tucked in the corner reading what looked like a mystery or thriller. He looked up and smiled and I was surprised to find that it was a little shy. Whenever we'd interacted doing wedding prep together for my brother, or at the wedding itself, he'd always been so self-confident, cocky even. I found I liked this softer side of him too.

'Morning,' he murmured, folding the page of his book and setting it down on the small table next to him as he walked over to me. I tensed slightly, we'd kissed last night, twice, but I wasn't sure what he was expecting now. Did he expect more kissing? More than that? Fletch interrupted my thoughts by wrapping his arms around me and pressing his face into my hair. 'I missed you,' he rumbled and I couldn't fight the smile that broke out as I returned the embrace.

'How could you have missed me if you were asleep?' I teased and the familiar cocky grin I was coming to like spread across his face.

'I didn't get much sleep,' he said suggestively and my face flushed hot.

'Oh,' I said faintly, trying to erase the mental image his words inspired, Fletcher panting in his bed, sheets spread and curled around his waist while his hand–

Fletcher chuckled knowingly as he swept a piece of his light hair out of his eyes. 'So I'm going to head down to the basement level to check out the fuse box, will you come with me? It might be dark so if you could hold a candle for me I'd appreciate it.'

'Of course,' I said, relieved to give my brain something else to focus on. We headed downstairs and I grabbed a long dining room candle and lit it with a match as we walked down the stairs to the basement. There was a small utility room on the far end of the corridor in the opposite direction to the sauna and close to one of the other many bedrooms this place had. There was another set of steps leading down and I led the way with the candle held aloft so we wouldn't trip or fall. The candle light barely penetrated the room and descending into darkness with Fletch felt electric, the sound of our breaths loud and his warmth at my back distracting.

'Over there,' Fletcher pointed and I directed the candle light so we could take a closer look at the big, dusty box attached to the wall. 'We were probably supposed to turn this on when we first arrived,' Fletch mused, 'but I bet Rob has all the check-in instructions and I just didn't think about it, I'm sorry.'

I shrugged, 'It's not your fault, I didn't think to check it either.'

Fletcher and I walked closer, dodging boxes and what looked like a spare hoover, and lifted the lid of the fuse box, pushing it out to the side, and we both winced at the creak that emerged. Considering how hi-tech this place was it was surprising that the fuse box was so old. Fletch must have been thinking the same thing because he cast me a wry look and said, 'Guess the snowstorms only emerge when we're planning a trip,' and I laughed lightly, moving closer to him to cast more light on the box and switches.

'Okay,' he said, 'I think maybe it's this one here–' he flicked the switch and a humming noise started. 'Ah, good. So, I flipped the fuse back and now let's turn on the back-ups in case the storm knocks it out again.' He reached for another switch just as a spark of electricity leapt up from the box and I screamed, jumping back. My arms pinwheeled and my legs tangled hopelessly as I tripped on a box behind me, dropping my candle as I attempted to catch myself.

Fletch caught the candle quickly, stamping out an errant curl of fire before it could spread, but I continued to fall until my head hit something solid with a *thunk* that made Fletcher's eyes dart up and widen in alarm before darkness swallowed me whole.

CHAPTER TWELVE

SARA

I was in a gently rocking boat, swaying from side to side. It was a surprisingly warm boat and come to think of it, I wasn't sure *why* I would be sailing. The last thing I could remember was Fletcher. We were in Alaska together at a lodge by the bay. He'd been looking at the fuse box when a spark had jumped and I–I couldn't really remember.

My eyes fluttered open to find two deep pools of blue staring down at me in a mixture of concern and panic. Fletch's face seemed oddly close to mine, I'd only seen him like this when we'd been about to kiss – was that what was happening now? I gave an airy giggle and let one hand flop up to rest against the faint stubble lining his jaw. Fletcher frowned and I patted the line between his eyebrows sloppily, the rocking stopped and I glanced about, shocked to find myself off of the ground and in Fletch's arms.

'Hello,' I said with another strange giggle, 'why am I so high up?'

Fletcher cursed, 'Sara, how are you feeling?'

Now that I thought about it, my head *did* throb quite a bit. Was that why Fletcher was carrying me? 'Ow,' I said, patting the large egg on the back of my head.

He sighed, 'Yeah that's what I thought.'

The rocking started up again as he carried me through the

lodge and into the lounge. I pressed my face into his chest, luxuriating in the warmth of his hands on my body and the smell of fabric softener and cologne in his jumper. Fletch sat on the sofa with me still in his lap and ran a gentle hand over my hair, reaching for one of the soft blankets I'd left downstairs with his free hand as he pulled it up and over us, tucking it in around me softly.

'You knocked yourself pretty good, gorgeous.'

'Didn't mean to,' I mumbled, the longer I was awake the more the odd hysteria faded and my head ached. His hand continued to stroke the length of my long hair and I sighed, relaxing into him. 'Thank you,' I said and his voice sounded surprised when he replied.

'For what?'

'Taking care of me.'

He chuckled deeply, 'Well I wasn't exactly going to leave you passed out in the basement.'

I ignored him, grateful for the fact that he cared enough to carry me up here in his arms – I was heavy, so I knew that had taken effort especially with all the stairs – cuddle me on the sofa and tuck me into a blanket. He pressed a hand to my forehead and hummed before peering into my eyes, my breath caught at the intense ocean-blue stare.

'I don't think you're concussed, but probably best you don't move for a while.'

'I have some painkillers in my wash bag upstairs, could you get it for me?' I hoped he'd say yes because despite the throb fading to a dull ache, I *really* did not want to move right now.

'Sure thing, gorgeous. You just stay right here, okay?'

I must have dozed off while he was gone because I woke up in a sweaty cocoon of blankets, spied some Tylenol on the side next to a large glass of water and I was once more in Fletch's arms as he stroked my back.

'Oh man, how long was I asleep for?'

'Couple hours,' his voice rumbled soothingly through his

chest and into mine and I smiled slightly as I pushed off some of the blankets. 'How do you feel?'

I touched the back of my head gingerly and gave a sigh of relief when the pain didn't make me want to puke, 'Actually, a lot better. I'd still like the meds though.' Fletcher nodded and passed them over, I gulped them down and then peered up at him curiously. 'Have you been sitting here this whole time, watching me sleep?'

A small blush stole over his cheeks and I stifled a grin, 'Okay, I wasn't *watching you sleep*. I was just making sure you were okay. Besides, I did leave for a little while.'

Disappointment flared up and I pushed it away, 'You did?'

His crooked grin flashed across his face, 'Yeah, I have a surprise for you. I was going to wait but I thought you would probably need them now more than ever.'

I looked at him in absolute confusion as he lifted me off his lap and strolled over to the kitchen. 'What are you doing?'

'You'll see,' he called and I could hear the laughter in his voice. He walked back in a moment later holding a plate and I gasped as he got close enough for me to see what was on it.

'You baked me cookies?'

He shrugged, 'Well, they were a packet mix, but yeah. I saw them in the shop and remembered how much you said you liked them when we were drunk at the wedding.'

I let out a loud laugh, 'Oh my God, I forgot about that.' I shook my head, mortified, I was pretty sure my exact words had been *Cookies are possibly better than sex, you know*. Of course, later on that night Fletch had definitely proved me wrong – not that I would tell him that.

I reached for one, perfectly golden, chocolate chip cookie and moaned when I bit into it. They were slightly gooey in the middle which, in my opinion, was the only way to have them.

'Thank you,' I said, smiling up at him and pecking him on the cheek as he sat down next to me on the sofa. He turned a little redder and I watched in fascination as the colour spread over his cheeks.

He nodded, eyes warm on mine, 'You're welcome.'

Silence followed but it was the comfortable kind while we munched on cookies and watched the fire crackle. By the time the plate was cleared I was feeling a lot better and Fletch stood up abruptly, tugging on his boots, scarf and coat while I watched with raised eyebrows.

'Is this a show opposite to the one you gave me the other night? Where you put more clothes on instead of taking them off?'

He laughed as he walked over to gently tug me off the sofa. 'Put your shoes and coat on.'

I did as he instructed but grimaced as he walked towards the door, 'You really want to go out there?'

'Trust me?' He asked, his hand outstretched and I didn't have to think about it before placing mine in his. His grin was so broad it made my heart stop before starting back up again at double speed.

It was surprisingly calm outside. The snow still poured down but the wind had eased and for a moment we just stared out at the white expanse, our breaths fogging the air around us.

'It's beautiful,' I said and he murmured an agreement, catching my hand in his again and moving just a little bit closer to my side before stepping away and throwing himself down into the snow at our feet. It puffed up in a powdery cloud and I shrieked. 'What are you doing?'

He was laughing as he looked up at me from the ground, 'Join me.'

I hesitated for a moment and then shrugged, why not? I folded myself down into the snow a little more gracefully and released a breath in a sigh as my head met the cold snow and it soothed the bump still high on my head.

'Are you ready?' he asked and I had no idea what he was talking about as he grabbed my hand in one of his and then spread his arms and legs out wide, raising an eyebrow to encourage me to do the same. I mimicked him and then laughed as he tugged my hand up and down, moving his legs in time, making slightly messy angels in the snow.

'You know, I don't think I've ever made a snow angel before,' I smiled as we lay there afterwards, staring up at the sky as snow drifted down onto our faces, tangling in our hair. The cold slowly seeped into me but I didn't mind, it wasn't until I started to shiver that Fletch stood and I followed suit. Our angels laid deep into the snow, interlinked at the arms and I turned to Fletcher with a smile, taking in the lightness of his eyes, the relaxed, happy look on his face.

I stepped a little closer and his gaze dropped to my mouth. I licked my lips and he looked like a man starved. Linking my arms around his neck, I pressed myself against him, shuddering as his heat warmed me.

'Can I kiss you?' he asked softly, the fog of our breath intertwining and his blue eyes deepening when I nodded. 'Thank fuck,' he gasped, bringing his hands up to clasp my face and lowering his lips to mine.

It was like all of our other kisses and yet somehow *more*. Maybe because I was actually sober this time, or maybe because something delicate and fragile was growing between us and I realised I wasn't scared to let it in any more. Fletch wasn't the person I'd thought he was after that morning I'd woken up alone – if anything, he was everything I'd hoped he could be and things I'd never even guessed at.

I pulled back from the kiss and his lips curled in the same soft smile I knew I was probably wearing too. His hand found mine as we walked the short distance back to the lodge and for the first time, I was grateful we'd been forced onto this trip together.

CHAPTER THIRTEEN

SARA

We knocked the snow off of our boots at the door and I shivered as Fletcher brushed snow off my shoulders, back and butt. I raised an eyebrow at him when I turned around and he looked at me with wide-eyed innocence, 'You had snow all over you,' he turned around and threw a grin over his shoulder. 'Do me?'

I knew his choice of words had been deliberate but I ignored them as I ran my hands over his back and ass, hearing him mutter a curse as I took my time.

'I think you got it all,' he said at last, turning around and grabbing my hands with a searing look in his eyes that made heat pool in my core. I grinned cheekily and walked into the lodge, relaxing as the warmth of the fire hit me. 'I'll go and make us some hot drinks.'

I called out my thanks and then jumped as the sound of my phone ringing reverberated around the lodge. The storm really must have been clearing up if I actually had signal again.

My feet pounded up the stairs to my room to try and reach it in time and I winced as the movement sent pain shooting through my head again, not for the first time in my life I wished I was less clumsy.

'Hello?' I answered quickly without checking the caller

ID and smiled as my brother's voice sounded on the other end of the phone.

'Sara! Glad I finally caught you,' Rob said and I pulled my phone away from my ear and saw I had three missed calls.

'Oh, sorry, I was out in the snow and didn't bring my phone. There's been no signal here the last couple days.'

'That's alright, I was just phoning because Tanya and I have managed to book another flight, so we should get in tomorrow morning!' He sounded excited but all I felt was a surprising surge of panic and disappointment. This would be mine and Fletcher's last night alone together.

'Oh,' I said, working to get some enthusiasm into my voice, 'that's great!'

'How've things been going there?'

There was an odd note in Rob's voice that I couldn't quite place but I shrugged it off as I answered, 'Yeah, it's been fine. Not much to do though, we lost power for a day or so.'

'Ah crap, that sucks. Well, anyway, we should be with you guys by late morning tomorrow I think–' a voice murmured in the background and Rob laughed, '–yeah, so we'll see you then. I've got to go... do something for Tanya.'

I grimaced, *newlyweds*. They weren't even subtle about it. 'Sure, safe flight. See you guys tomorrow.'

I hung up feeling a little deflated. I'd expected to hate every second of this trip, but once Fletch and I had cleared the air between us I'd actually been having a good time – head injuries notwithstanding. More than just being here in the lodge though, I'd had a good time with *Fletch* and, if I was being honest with myself, I couldn't think of anyone else I'd rather have been here with.

'Hot chocolates are ready!' Fletcher called from downstairs and I called back as I dropped my phone to the bed and made my way back to him. 'Were you on the phone?' he asked as I drew closer and accepted a mug.

'Yeah,' I said glumly, 'Rob and Tanya have managed to

get a new flight now the storm is passing. They'll be here tomorrow.'

Fletch looked at me hesitantly, 'That's... great?'

'I guess.'

'Is there a reason you sound so–'

'Depressed?' I tried to laugh but it came out a little strangled. 'I–I've been having fun spending time with you, Fletch, and when they arrive, things will change.'

His face softened and he lowered his mug from his mouth as he bridged the space between us. 'I've enjoyed it too, but that doesn't have to stop as soon as we walk out of the door to head home you know.'

I sucked in a breath, 'It doesn't?'

'No,' he smiled. 'In fact, I really hope it doesn't. I like you and I think that you might like me.'

'Maybe,' I said with a smirk and he laughed. I blew gently on my hot chocolate as I glanced down at it and froze. 'Fletcher, what's that on the top?'

It smelled good, rich and chocolatey, and he'd stirred it just the right amount to have plenty of foam sitting on top and a sprinkle of something else.

'Oh, it's just something I do when I make hot chocolate. Just a small pinch of the powder and–'

'–sprinkle it on top,' I whispered, staring at him with my eyes wide because I did the *exact same thing* and Rob had always thought it was gross as hell. I didn't make a conscious decision, I just knew right then that whatever it was that burned between me and Fletcher, I wanted more of it.

'Sara, I–' he looked so confused as I moved two steps closer and stretched up to capture his mouth with mine. He groaned and mumbled something against my lips that I didn't quite catch as I crushed myself against him, letting my hot chocolate fall forgotten to the hardwood floor as I sank my hands into his hair and jumped up to wrap my legs around his waist.

'*Fuck,*' he growled as he fumbled to set his own drink

down before giving up and catching the underside of my thighs and pressing himself into me through my sweats. Hot chocolate flew and I caught a droplet on his cheek with my tongue, licking it away and enjoying the fire that started in his eyes as he reclaimed my mouth with a hard kiss. Fletcher captured my lip between his teeth and bit down, tugging on it lightly before deepening the kiss so his tongue brushed mine.

My sweatshirt had a thorough coating of chocolate and Fletch tugged on the hem as he walked us back towards the dining room table and laid me down. 'I think this needs to come off,' he said with a wicked grin as he pushed it up and kissed and licked a trail of heat up from my stomach to my breasts. I panted as he neared one arch but he pulled away after leaving me with one lingering kiss to the underside of each of my breasts. Fletch slid the jumper up and over my head, throwing it down somewhere out of sight and I shivered as the air brushed my skin, exposed on the table. It was a good thing we were in the middle of nowhere because if somebody were to walk past those windows right now they would be getting one hell of a show.

Fletch stood in between my legs as he lowered his body against mine, rocking his hips slightly with his eyes fluttering closed. They quickly flashed open though as he pulled himself away. 'No, no,' he murmured as I whimpered, 'this is going to be all about you.'

I pouted and opened my mouth only to moan as he pulled one nipple into his mouth, flicking his tongue over the tip and sending a bolt of heat straight to my clit. One of his hands slid down from my hip to my thigh and I shifted against him restlessly, impatient, but he just pinched my ass in admonishment and moved to my other breast. He devoured me while I writhed before him, needing more, craving relief from the pressure slowly building.

Instead he continued working me into a frenzy with his tongue and teeth, sucking and nipping at my breasts while he teased the other with his hand.

'Fletcher, *please,*' I said and his hand at last smoothed down my stomach and then paused, flirting with the edge of my waistband. I made a sound of pure frustration and sent my own hand down, intent on getting myself where I needed to be if he wouldn't. Fletch caught my hand with a slow tut, pushing it back and over my head and then capturing the other when I attempted the same.

His face showed nothing but satisfaction as he watched me spread before him, pinned and at his mercy. A searing kiss was pressed to my lips as he finally tugged my joggers down. Then he swore.

'Don't tell me,' he said roughly, voice husky and tight like he was having trouble controlling himself, 'that this entire time you've been bare, gorgeous.'

I smirked as I tilted my hips up and down, begging him to touch me without saying a word. 'I forgot to pack my panties.'

He watched the movement of my hips as though hypnotised, 'I'm going to taste you now,' he said, sinking to his knees and releasing my arms, 'and if you're good I'll let you come on my tongue.'

His words made me clench and I felt my slickness growing. He looked up at me from between my thighs, his mouth just a breath away from me, 'Would you like that, gorgeous? To ride my face?'

I nodded with a pant and he shook his head slowly as he traced one finger over my pussy, ghosting over my clit and he pressed down as he asked, 'No, I'm going to need to hear it.'

'I want to ride your face,' I moaned and without another word his mouth closed over me, tongue lapping gently before plunging down and dipping inside of me, mouth sucking at my clit and my hips jerked up instinctively. '*Fletcher.*'

'I love it when you say my name,' he murmured, eyes glazed as he worked a finger into me and bent his head to taste me again. 'Now, I'm going to make you scream it.'

CHAPTER FOURTEEN

FLETCHER

Sara had a glazed look on her face and I couldn't stop my smirk as I looked at her, spread out on the dining room table for me like my own personal feast. When we'd had sex before, it had been great, but we were both drunk and rushing but now… I was going to take my time.

'I hope you're not too worn out already,' I teased her, sliding a finger back into her warm wetness and sucking on it when I pulled it out, loving the way she watched me with her lips parted and eyes wide. She widened her legs for me and I bit back a groan – Sara was unbelievably sexy and I didn't think she was even trying. I slid a hand up and over the creamy, soft skin of her stomach and up to her full breasts, cupping them in my palms as I stroked a thumb across each dusky pink nipple. 'Because there's a lot more that I want us to cover tonight – but Sara, I meant it before. There's no rush, this between us isn't going to suddenly go away just because we leave the lodge.'

She pulled herself into a seated position, breasts pressed flush against my chest as she looked into my eyes. 'I want everything,' she said, voice husky from how loudly I'd made her moan just moments ago. 'I want you.' Then she kissed me, her lips warm and firm and teasing as they nipped at me, her tongue twining expertly around mine.

I pulled my jumper over my head and shuddered at the feel of her hands on my bare skin, stroking my chest, kissing her way down and stroking me through the material of my pants. I took her hand in mine and kissed it, 'I want to last,' I joked and she grinned in a way that had me hardening almost painfully.

We moved back over to the sofa, stepping carefully to avoid the splotches of hot chocolate on the floor that we'd have to clean up later. Luckily the cups had been a solid plastic and there wasn't anything sharp in the way of our path.

Sara lowered herself to her knees with her back to the fireplace and I let her slip a hand under my waistband and pull down the bottoms, enjoying the way she gasped as my dick sprang out, already hard for her.

I slid my hand around my base and pumped once, twice, her eyes watching me with an intensity that had me near exploding. She licked her lips slowly and I knew what she wanted. It would feel incredible to have her lips around me again – that part of our drunken night stood out for me very vividly – but it would feel *too* good and then neither of us would get the ending we really wanted. So I sank down onto my knees in front of her and kissed her, my dick bobbed, brushing against her stomach and sending small ripples of pleasure through me at the contact.

'Another time,' I promised and she pushed those gorgeous lips out into a pout that had me reconsidering for half a second until I shook the thought away. I grabbed a few of the pillows from the sofa, as well as the blanket we'd been wrapped in earlier, and laid them on the floor. Without taking her eyes off of me, Sara sank down onto the pile, her chest arched upwards, skin aglow in the firelight.

I crawled over to her and lifted one of her legs, kissing my way up her calf and onto her inner thigh, loving the way she panted and moaned for me. I sent a hand over her pussy, feeling her wetness on the tips of my fingers and cursing as I fought the need to immediately sink inside her. My hips flexed and she sent one hand down my stomach until she grasped me firmly, giving me a couple of experimental strokes before finding her rhythm.

'Sara–' I moaned, fuck, I would be slower next time but now I just needed to be inside her. I coaxed in one finger and then slid another into her, pumping in and out as she writhed beneath me, her head tilted back and soft cries escaping her plush mouth. Her hand hesitated on me as she got caught up in the sensation and I pressed my thumb to her clit, wanting her to be as close to the edge as I was. 'Oh fuck,' I said as a thought occurred to me, 'I don't suppose you packed any condoms?'

She let out a breathy laugh of incredulity, 'Yeah, I forgot my panties but I definitely packed condoms for the trip I was supposed to be taking with my brother and his wife.'

'A simple *no* would have sufficed,' I said with a little smirk and she continued to peer up at me, absolute faith in her eyes.

'I'm on the pill,' she said eventually, 'I haven't been with anyone except Zach recently and we used a condom, I get tested regularly so I'm clean. If… you're okay with it then I am too?'

Sweat was breaking out on the bottom of my back as I breathed a sigh of relief at her words, 'I haven't been with anyone since you and I get checked regularly too. God, I'm so glad you're on the pill.'

She gave a laugh and her hand began to move over me again, making my eyes close and head tip back as I let her draw me closer. I rubbed at her warm entrance, giving a low moan at the feel of her silkiness against me, her hands were against her boobs and for a moment I just admired her as I pressed myself against her in long, slow strokes.

'Sara,' I said and she opened her eyes to look at me, I pressed my finger to her clit, rubbing it in time with my strokes. 'I want you to scream my name again. I want mine to be the only name you ever scream.' I let the head of my dick rub her clit before sliding all the way back down again and moving inside of her slowly, inch by inch, and she squirmed and sighed as she rocked her hips to try to take me in further. 'Tell me you're mine.'

'I'm yours.'

I filled her all the way and continued to stroke her with my hand and little whimpers spilled from her lips that nearly undid me. 'Are you ready to scream for me?' Sara moaned and I thrust in and out in one quick, hard motion. 'Tell me, gorgeous.'

'I'm going to scream for you, Fletcher.'

I lost it as she said my name, grabbing her leg and bringing it over my shoulder and pressing into her deeply. She cried out and I increased my pace, reaching for her breasts with one hand and then leaning forward to taste her moans on my tongue. I moved back, breathing hard, and lowered her leg before sitting back and tugging her towards me and riding her while she gasped for more. I reached between us and sent my fingers over her clit as I moved inside her and her breathing quickened, her moans became deeper and I lifted her onto my lap so we were pressed tightly together.

Not an inch of space separated us as we ground against one another and my name quickly became the only thing passing her lips.

'I want to ride you,' she groaned, '*Fletcher*, please.'

I leaned back and let her legs fall to either side of me, she pressed a palm to my chest and her hair made a curtain between us and the rest of the room as she pressed herself down and onto me over and over.

'*Fletcher!*'

'Sara – tell me–'

'I'm yours,' she moaned and I felt her tighten around me as her orgasm took over and I called her name as I fell apart with her.

Once our heartbeats had slowed, I rolled her off of me and tucked her into my side where she fit perfectly.

'That was...'

'It *definitely* happened.'

'You are so cheesy and I love it. I really am sorry about that note, I was still drunk and it made sense at the time,' I laughed as I ran a hand down her arm, content in hearing her breaths and filling my nose with her familiar smell.

'You're an idiot,' she said and I could practically hear her eyes rolling, 'but I forgive you.'

'I'm glad. Truly. Now we just have to hope that Rob will forgive me too for fucking you not just once – but twice.'

'I'm not sure it's any of his business,' Sara said, propping herself up and looking at me with a raised eyebrow.

I laughed, 'Well, I am his best friend, a heads-up would probably have been nice for him.'

Sara nodded, 'Yeah, okay, fair point – I know you guys have 'bro code' or whatever. But…'

'Yeah?'

'Well, we've already had sex twice now. What's one more time going to hurt, really?'

I grinned at her, 'You're insatiable.'

She shrugged but gave me a coy smile, 'You're good in bed and I think we should be making the most of our last night alone together here.'

'You are absolutely right,' I said, reaching out and snagging her around the waist, 'it would be rude not to.'

'My thoughts exactly,' she said huskily and I pressed a kiss to her lips as she sank her fingers into my hair.

CHAPTER FIFTEEN

SARA

I was still tired when I woke up the next morning. My muscles were pleasantly sore and the gentle sound of Fletcher's breathing in my ear made me smile sleepily. We'd stayed up most of the night talking and laughing and having a *lot* of sex. Like, at some point I'd thought I'd run out of energy or that he'd finally be satisfied, but we had mostly passed out from sheer necessity rather than the want to stop.

I gave a long stretch and Fletch's arm tightened around my bare stomach. We'd made a sort of fort on the sofa with pillows and blankets and had wound up falling asleep there – having sex in a bedroom again was going to feel like a novelty the next time we did it. The thought filled me with a purr of satisfaction – Fletcher *wanted me*. I hated that we'd lost out on time just because of a misunderstanding and one day I knew we would laugh about it the way we'd started to last night.

'While I'm thrilled to see you two getting along together, I do wish I wasn't seeing quite so much of you both right now.'

My eyes flew open. *No*. How had we forgotten? This was possibly not the best way to break the news to my brother that I was sleeping with his best friend.

We were dead. Rob was going to blow a fuse any second and kill us both. Well, at least, definitely me because I was sure he'd find a way to make this all my fault. I loved my brother, really, I did – but nine times out of ten he treated me like I was still ten-years-old.

Fletch cursed, sitting upright quickly and attempting to hide my very naked body behind his. 'Rob–' Fletcher apparently didn't know what else to say and to be honest, I didn't either. When we'd spoken briefly before about what – and when – we'd tell my brother, it had always involved the both of us being fully clothed in a room that probably didn't smell like a sex-fest had just occurred.

Rob and Tanya stood in the entryway, their bags on the floor at their feet. Tanya looked amused and Rob looked... not angry? It was hard to tell though, my brother had always been described as *classically handsome,* but I thought that was mostly code for *emotionless robot*. Seriously, he could make a killing at poker if he tried, his poker face was that good. That's why his relationship with Tanya always baffled me, she was fun, bright, *cheerful*. I guess it was true what they said – opposites really did attract.

'So... how was your flight?' I said and Rob raised his eyebrow but didn't comment on my obvious diversion tactic.

'Good, I guess you forgot we were coming in early?'

'Ah yes,' I mumbled and Tanya giggled before hiding it behind a cough.

The silence stretched on until Rob sighed. 'Look, Tan and I will find ourselves a room for our bags and you two can get... presentable.' With that, he turned and walked up the stairs, their overnight bags in hand and shoulders tense. Tanya gave me a broad grin and the sight of her cheery pink afro-curls made me relax a little as I shot her a small little wave in between grappling for the blanket to keep myself covered.

When she was out of sight I turned to Fletcher with wide eyes, he was reclining on the sofa with the blanket covering his lap and his hands over his eyes. I could hear Tanya giggling somewhere upstairs and my mouth opened and closed like a fish.

'I can't believe this is happening,' I said and Fletcher gave a low sound of agreement that shouldn't have turned me on but did.

He removed his hands from his face and looked at me like he knew exactly what filthiness was occurring in my thoughts and I blushed.

'I can't hear you moving!' Rob called and I pulled a face as I mimicked him.

'Sorry, *Mom,*' I yelled back and heard Tanya shushing him. I grinned, I'd won that round at least – but it felt like Rob had won the war after catching me with my literal pants down. 'Is it just me, or did he seem pretty... calm, to you?'

Fletcher winced, 'Maybe he's saving his rage for when we're both dressed. It's not very sporting to beat up a naked man.'

I laughed, 'My brother will not beat you up. You could totally take him, plus, Tanya won't let him.'

Fletcher grinned at that and I wrapped one blanket carefully around myself as I tugged him up with a roll of my eyes. 'Come on, let's go and get dressed before he has a hissy fit.'

Fletcher and I had showered together, 'To save time,' I'd argued. He'd just grinned and climbed in and by the time we came back down again, Rob and Tanya were waiting.

My brother's face was as coolly impassive as usual and I shot Tanya a questioning look to try and work out how worried I needed to be, she gave a light shrug in response. Great. Rob held my coat out to me, 'I thought it might be nice for us to all go for a walk to the lake, now that it's safe to leave here again. Not–' he muttered under his breath, 'that it looked like you two were having much trouble staying occupied.'

I shrugged my puffer coat on and my eyes met Fletcher's as we walked out of the front door. 'Do you think he's going to murder us and dump the bodies in the lake?'

'Don't be silly,' Rob said from behind me and I jumped, 'the lake is still frozen.'

I wasn't sure whether or not that was a comfort.

It was nice to get out of the lodge, just me, Fletch and... my brother. Tanya had stayed behind in the warmth, waving us off after claiming she felt a little nauseous, and I looked behind regretfully, half-wishing I'd done the same. Except, that would leave Fletcher alone with Rob and that did not seem like a wise (or fair) decision right now.

Rob had the right idea though, it was almost mild outside – or as mild as Alaska in the snow could be – it was snowing very lightly and I pulled my gloves out of my coat pocket and slipped them on. I wanted to move closer to Fletcher, huddle in his warmth and share a kiss to chase away the cold. My brother cleared his throat and I realised I'd been stuck in place, staring at Fletcher for a couple seconds too long. My face burned as I quickly moved forward to join them, there were footprints in the snow and that brought me a little relief because it meant that there would be other people out at the lake, saving me from an otherwise awkward excursion. Plus, Rob couldn't murder us if there were witnesses, right?

The lake was beautiful. It was completely frozen over and a few people were ice-skating over on the far left ahead of us but I hesitated on the edge.

'It's definitely safe, right?'

Fletcher wordlessly offered me a hand and I threw a cautious look Rob's way before taking it and letting him lead me out. It wasn't too slippery, surprisingly, most of the ice was covered in snow, so we could walk out and enjoy the view of the mountain face opposite and the copse of fir trees capped with white. Fletcher's hand was warm through my cotton gloves and I smiled at him. It was funny really that I'd thought Fletch looked the part of Cali-boy before, but here on the lake I realised he looked more at home against the backdrop of the snow.

I could feel Rob's eyes on us as we walked around the lake,

chatting and laughing and I raised my head to look at him challengingly. My brother and I used to get along amazingly, and sometimes we still did, but more and more I felt like he saw me as a problem or a burden to be carried. Doing wedding prep together was the first time in a long time that it seemed like he'd seen me for me and not the teenager he remembered.

'Does he seem a little too chilled out to you?' I asked Fletcher in a low undertone and he glanced back to where Rob stood, taking a photo of the snow on his iPhone before making a noncommittal hum. 'I mean, if you had a sister and Rob went behind your back and slept with her, wouldn't you want to tear his head off? Or am I just being paranoid?'

'Maybe he's just hiding it really well,' Fletch suggested with a quirk of his lips.

'Rob passing up on a chance to ridicule me and my life choices? I don't know... Quick, he's coming over, put your arms around my waist!' Fletcher looked startled but immediately did so and I relaxed into the warmth of his arms as my brother came to stand next to us.

Rob tilted his head, 'so, what, are you guys a couple now or something?'

And just like that, my brother took the upper hand once more. I looked to Fletcher, his face unnervingly close to mine and he looked at me. I licked my lips and he cleared his throat as we both looked at each other and then away. This was not a conversation we'd managed to have yet after only just deciding to do... whatever it was we had done last night. Here Rob was, charging in and asking us right here and now to define the relationship. I shot him a glare and he looked at me as if he couldn't imagine what I was upset about.

Then Fletch's hand closed over my hip, the warmth sending a bolt of desire through me and I looked up at him in surprise.

'Yeah man, if you're cool with it I think that's where this is headed – I need to take her out on a proper date first though.' Fletcher's eyes were warm as they met mine and I bit my lip to stop the smile from overtaking my face. *Okay, so maybe Rob didn't quite win that one.*

I gave a quick laugh at the brief look of surprise that sped across my brother's face, 'Yeah I guess Rob and Tanya's wedding doesn't really count as much of a first date.' As soon as the words were out I wanted to kick myself, the widening of Fletch's eyes told me I'd made a mistake and the small frown twisting Rob's mouth made me feel ill as I waited for his response.

My brother was many things, but stupid wasn't one of them. He took in the look of horror on Fletch's face and the abject guilt likely written across mine and let out a deep breath, his nostrils flaring. 'This,' he said, gesturing between the two of us, 'Didn't just happen for the first time in the lodge, did it. That's why you were mopey after the wedding, Fletch, and why you were acting like you were heartbroken by that guy you met-up with like one time. God, at my wedding?' Rob shook his head but still didn't seem as mad as I had expected. 'Could you two be any more of a cliche? I mean, the groomsman and the maid of honour?'

A lick of anger made its way through my body and I suddenly couldn't hold back any of my old hurt as his condescending words hit me. 'Huh, that's *so* funny Rob, because I'm actually just trying to recall when I asked for your opinion. Or why you'd think I care about it. God knows you've proved over and over that you think you're so much better than me, so why bother inviting me on this trip in the first place? Just so you can make me feel more inadequate?'

Rob's dark eyes were wide and Fletcher's hand squeezed mine as I blinked away a stupid rush of tears and shook my head. 'I'm going back to the lodge.'

'I'll come with you,' Fletch said gently and I couldn't look at him, knowing the soft, pitying look he was probably wearing would only cause the tears to come back and I didn't want to cry, damnit, I was *mad*.

Rob followed us at a sedate pace and the short walk back

to the lodge was silent except for our heavy, chilled breaths and the crunch of the snow under our feet.

Tanya had clearly spotted us coming from one of the windows and met us at the door, the big smile on her face withering as she took in our expressions. We knocked the snow off our boots without a word and my eyes fell to the patch of floor that had still been sticky with hot chocolate when we'd left. It looked like Tanya had cleaned it up and I gave her a grateful smile as I hung up my coat and sat down in front of the fireplace.

Someone sat down next to me on the sofa and I turned around, expecting it to be Fletcher, but it was Rob. I immediately twisted myself back to face the fire, not having anything more to say to him.

'I didn't know you felt that way,' he said eventually, 'that I *made* you feel that way. I'm nothing but proud of you, Sara. You're my sister and I just... I just wanted what was best for you.'

I felt some of the ice coating my heart crack and I let loose a sigh, 'You have a terrible way of showing it.'

'Yeah Tanya says I need to work on being more 'emotive'.'

I burst out laughing and he joined in, the sound ringing strangely but comfortingly and I relaxed into his side.

'Hey,' Tanya said, coming over and standing next to the sofa. 'We bought supplies for the lodge on the way, so I made us all grilled cheeses.'

My stomach grumbled loudly and I beamed, standing up and kissing Tanya on the cheek as I made my way to the dining table. 'I'm so glad my brother married you, Tan.'

She let out a peel of laughter as she strode off to the kitchen and Rob caught my hand before I could completely pass him.

'In the spirit of honesty,' he said, face back to its characteristic solemnity but the twitch of his eye betrayed his nervousness for once, 'I have something I need to tell you. And Fletcher.'

My heart thudded a little faster. Was he going to give us

his blessing? Not that I really felt that we needed it, we were grown adults and Rob didn't own me *or* Fletcher. Or maybe he was about to tell us he hated the idea of us together.

Rob stood and made his way to the table, sitting down in one of the chairs just as Fletcher came down the stairs. 'I already knew about what happened at the wedding between the two of you.'

CHAPTER SIXTEEN

SARA

I stared at Rob, too distracted for a moment by the memory of what Fletch and I had done on the exact spot my brother now had his elbow resting on to really hear what he was saying.

'Yeah, because we told you, like twenty minutes ago,' I said, a beat late.

Fletcher caught the blush that was working its way across my cheeks and smirked as he followed my gaze. Rob looked between us and the table before pulling his arm away like it was on fire, grimacing as he asked, 'Do I even want to know?'

Fletcher clapped him on the back and took a seat next to him on one side of the table, I took the place opposite and Tanya slid in next to me, setting grilled cheese toasties down in front of each of us.

Rob took a breath as if to steady himself and that made me pay attention, Rob was *never* unsure – but I guessed we were both learning new things about each other today. 'No, I mean, I've known since the day after the wedding.'

Silence descended and the bite of toast in my mouth suddenly felt like cotton as I struggled to swallow. 'You *what*? Why didn't you say something?'

Rob raised an eyebrow cooly, 'Well, neither of you seemed inclined to bring it up either.'

Okay, point. 'But out on the lake you acted like you were surprised and I don't–'

My eyes widened as a thought occurred to me. Rob's lack of anger or concern, the fact that he apparently knew what had happened between me and Fletcher *before* he'd invited us on this trip– 'were you trying to *Parent Trap* us?' My voice had risen shrilly and Tanya patted my shoulder comfortingly. Had she known too?

Fletcher rubbed at his eyes tiredly, 'What, dare I ask, is a Parent Trap?'

'He set us up,' I accused and Rob didn't even try to deny it.

'You were both being idiots, pining after each other without knowing the full story. It was driving me crazy. I waited, I swear I waited, because I thought, *surely these two people who I care about a lot wouldn't be so stupid as to let this opportunity pass them by*. But a week turned into two and you were both clearly unhappy and *lying* to me about it.'

Anger was washing through me too fiercely for me to listen to him right now. I stood abruptly but Fletcher reached across the table and laid a comforting hand on my shoulder. I sat back down and Fletcher walked to the kitchen, the now-familiar sound of him opening and closing cupboards drained some of my tension away and I let out a slow breath as he set a cup of tea in front of me and gestured to the pot for Rob and Tanya.

'So what was your plan? Get us here and ditch us?' I looked accusingly at the newlyweds and Tanya looked a little remorseful while Rob just took in my anger resolutely.

'No, I just wanted you to spend more time together, maybe force some team-building activities. To be honest, I hoped you'd sort it out between you on the car ride over.'

My mouth dropped open, having forgotten about that small detail, and my fists curled as I realised Rob would have known just how uncomfortable he was making us by getting in the car together.

'The snowstorm came in handy, I guess,' he continued mildly and by that point I'd had enough.

'Honey, we just wanted you both to be happy,' Tanya chipped in and I could only stare at her. 'I told him that he might not get the results he wanted if he interfered, but you know your brother can be a little... single-minded.' I appreciated Tanya's attempt to be diplomatic and that Rob was her husband, but we'd started to become friends before the wedding. That she hadn't even attempted to give me a heads-up about what my brother had been planning stung almost as much as Rob's meddling.

'I can't believe you let him think this was a good idea. You can't honestly tell me you fully agreed with this madness,' I rolled my eyes at her silence. Tan was too nice to be a good liar and she looked away quickly, messing with her nose ring and tugging at her pink ringlets.

'Yeah... ' I said slowly, 'that's what I thought.'

'Except for the fact it did work,' Rob pointed out. Fletcher's brows furrowed and he inched away from my brother as we both stared him down. Rob sighed and put down his cup, running a hand through his dark hair and levelling his dark eyes on me, 'You just needed a push and I wanted to help.'

'Lying to us was you trying to help?'

'Hello – pot, kettle,' Rob said, gesturing between me and Fletch.

I shrugged off his words even if he did have a point. 'How did you even know about it if neither of us told you? You and Tanya left the reception earlier than we did.'

'Fletcher told me what happened between you two almost as soon as it happened.'

I shot an outraged look at Fletch but he was already shaking his head, 'No, I didn't.'

My brother pinched the bridge of his nose and Tanya looked like she was maybe trying not to laugh and I nudged her, 'Yes, you did, Fletch. You were passed out in front of the elevator and I woke you up. I figured you didn't remember our conversation when you never brought up what happened again with me.'

It was a sweet relief to have that final confirmation from Rob that Fletch's story had been true – I'd believed him, but it was a comfort all the same.

'I don't remember talking to you,' Fletcher said, his blue eyes meeting mine in a panic and I gave him a reassuring smile to show I trusted him.

'I asked you why you were asleep outside of the lift and you said it was because you had slept with Sara but needed to talk to me before you could ask her out,' Rob rolled his eyes and to be honest, I was with him on that. What sort of assbackward– 'You were obviously still ridiculously drunk and of course I was shocked and maybe a little mad that you hadn't told me you liked her beforehand, but to be honest, in hindsight it made sense. Whenever she was in the room your eyes would gravitate to her and at every opportunity you were whisking her off to dance or touching her. You were head over heels.'

Fletcher was blushing and I was baffled, had I really been so clueless? It honestly hadn't been until near the end of the night that I'd got up the courage to ask Fletcher to bed and even then I'd been half-sure he was going to say no.

'But then you never brought it up again and Tanya told me that she had seen Sara running to Kate's room in floods of tears that morning, obviously I put two and two together and realised Sara thought she'd been ditched–'

'Well to be fair, he did leave a note,' I said defensively and Tanya nodded her head empathetically after looking at me with wide eyes, her fingers reaching out and squeezing mine tightly, and I considered that maybe she'd felt a little hurt that I hadn't confessed any of this to her either.

'I watched you both mope for almost a month and then I decided to book the lodge.'

I felt like my eyes couldn't get any wider at this point, 'So instead of speaking to the two of us and explaining the full-story, you tried to meddle in our lives and force us to get together?'

Tanya was looking a little nervous now as she patted my hand faster and faster, 'Well, you're not always so easy to talk to, we thought it would be easier to simply give you two the opportunity to work things out in a supervised setting. Then when we heard about the storm...'

'It was a gift horse,' Rob finished and I shook my head in disbelief.

'I can't believe you manipulated us like that, you–you're fucking *crazy*,' I could feel my skin flushing in anger and Fletcher looked at me in concern. For a second I was worried he was going to take their side too but he just shook his head.

'You shouldn't have messed about with us like that, man. We're not puppets.'

Rob half-shrugged, 'Well it seemed to work out alright for the two of you in the end though, didn't it?'

Outraged, I flew to my feet, 'The only thing you directly accomplished here was making me trust you even less than I already did. And I can't believe *you* let him go ahead with this!' Tanya and I had become somewhat close while I helped her with wedding prep and to know that she'd gone behind my back to try to control us like this was just...

Rob opened his mouth but I shook my head. 'This just proves more than ever what you really think of me. You're so full of shit, Rob, *I didn't know I made you feel like that* – I›m calling bullshit, otherwise you wouldn›t have tried to set this all up. You›d have just come and talked to me like a normal person.› I waved away his protests and stomped upstairs to collect my stuff.

A moment later Fletch came into my room and almost got hit by a bra that was thrown in my packing frenzy. He caught it and gave me a wry smile before it fell away, leaving a more serious expression in its place, 'I'm coming with you.'

A wave of relief swept through me so fiercely that for a second all I could do was stare at him before I walked over and he swept me into a tight hug.

'I'm sorry–'

'Rob's an ass–'

We stopped and laughed quietly together for a second before I pulled back to look at him.

'Will you come back to mine with me?' he asked hesitantly, lower lip caught between his teeth as he waited for my answer.

'I'd love that,' I smiled, I felt like I didn't know nearly as much as I wanted to about him yet and as we were cutting this trip short I still had a couple vacation days left off of work. 'There's no place I'd rather be... but maybe we could stop at mine so I can grab some panties?'

Fletch's eyes instantly heated, 'Oh, I don't think that'll be necessary.'

Well, on the one hand, Rob was unlikely to try and kick my ass for sleeping with his sister. Twice. I wasn't sure how to feel really. My oldest friend had not only betrayed me, but had used information I'd drunkenly provided to control my life. Sure, it had sort of turned out well, but it didn't excuse his methods.

I was glad Sara wanted to come back to my apartment with me, I'd been half-scared she was going to run at the first opportunity, maybe be the one to leave me a note this time as a little piece de resistance. But she wanted me. Wanted to explore whatever it was that was still simmering between us and considering how often that ache led to me stripping her bare, it was likely a good thing we would be leaving the lodge – and her brother – behind.

I moved around the room I'd claimed as my own for the past few days and gathered up a few toiletries, it felt like I'd barely slept in here when in reality it was only really the one night that Sara and I had curled up together. Soon she would be in my bed, hopefully naked and shouting my name.

I tried to imagine her in my apartment, curled up on my sofa, naked on my kitchen counter... I shook my head to clear those thoughts, as if my brain was an etch-a-sketch to be emptied at will. I found it easy, thinking about all the ways Sara could slot into my life, and hopefully vice versa. Seeing her laugh every day, waking up to red hair in my face in the mornings... I wish we could have enjoyed our first morning *together* before Rob and Tanya had shown up. But there would be time to make-up for that and I hoped it might lead to every morning together. I smiled at the thought as I pushed some errant pyjama bottoms into my bag. *Sara Bridges, you're going to be mine.*

CHAPTER SEVENTEEN

SARA

Our bags were packed in record time and Fletch carried them downstairs and out to the rental Rob and Tanya had driven to the lodge. He cast his truck a mournful look as he walked by and it tugged at my heart a little. Now the signal was back he had someone coming to siphon out the fuel, but in the meantime we had decided to take Rob's car until Fletch's was in drivable condition again.

Tanya stood by the front door, her kind eyes worried and her hands clasped tightly together as she tried to persuade us to stay. She looked a little pale but only smiled when I asked if she was alright. 'I'm okay, just feeling a little sick still, I'm probably just tired from traveling.' She caught my hand and gave it a gentle squeeze. 'I'm sorry, I should have told you what Rob was planning. He just made a bad call. You guys should stay, we can talk this out.'

I shook my head, 'I get why you went along with it, but I can't say it didn't hurt that you went behind my back. Rob, I expect stupid shit like this from. He hasn't even apologised, Tan, and his head is perpetually so far up his own ass that I doubt he will.'

Tanya moved a step closer to me and her soft jasmine perfume enveloped me in a soothing cloud, 'He's just stubborn, sort of like someone else I know.' She gave me a pointed look that I ignored as I slipped on my coat and boots.

'Look, I just need some time, okay?'

Tanya gave a tight but firm nod, her curls bouncing with the movement and my shoulders slumped as I pulled her in for a quick hug before walking away.

Fletch held the passenger side open for me and I climbed in with a flash of a smile in his direction – despite the crazy whirlwind that had been this afternoon, I had still found time to reminisce about last night while I packed. I didn't know where things with Fletcher would go, but I was excited to find out and to see his place. I was also pretty pleased that the sex was just as good as I remembered, I had been worried I'd overhyped him in my head, put him onto some untouchable pedestal. But no, he really was that good. Or rather, *we* were.

The rental was comfortable, the seats were heated and I sighed as I relaxed back into them as Fletcher shut his door, sealing out the cold. Here we were, several days later, trapped in a car together again – except now, I was more than happy to have the alone time.

Fletch seemed inclined to agree, 'So, my place then?'

I smiled as he reached for the aux cord, 'sounds good. I feel like I know you so well without really even knowing much about you.'

He raised an eyebrow at me as Taylor Swift came rolling out of the speakers, 'And you think seeing my place is going to help with that?'

'You can tell a lot about a person from the state of their underwear drawer,' I grinned and he let out a chuckle before turning to me with want written across his face.

'It's very forward of you to assume you'll get to see my underwear drawer.'

'Oh, we're just going straight to your sex dungeon then?' I widened my eyes innocently and burst out laughing when he blushed a little.

'Don't tempt me,' he said and I laughed again, falling

quiet as we began driving along the winding roads to take us back to Anchorage. In all honesty, I was worried about what Fletch's apartment would be like. I knew he lived fairly centrally, so it had to be modern, but was he a secret slob? Did all of his furniture match or did he even have any at all? You just couldn't tell what you would be getting with people these days.

There was a lot less snow and wind during the journey this time around and the tension present was of a very different kind. *Well*, I mused as I watched the muscles in Fletch's arm flex on the wheel, *maybe not that different*.

'Sara,' Fletcher said warningly and I snapped my gaze up from his chest to his face as he smirked at me. 'If you keep looking at me like that then this ride is going to get a little uncomfortable for me,' he looked meaningfully down at his pants.

'I'd say I'm sorry but I'm not,' I forced down a laugh and turned my gaze to the window instead, letting my eyes rest on the snow-topped trees and the mountain in the distance. It was the furthest thing from the Californian heat I'd grown up with, but I found it calming all the same. There was just something about the snow and ice at this time of year that was endlessly peaceful –

A warm hand landed on my thigh and sent a tingle of anticipation through me, tightening my nipples. I looked up at Fletcher with raised eyebrows and he sighed, 'The only thing worse than you eye-fucking me is you *not* eye-fucking me.'

I burst out laughing, 'I'm not even sure what that means, but know I plan on doing quite a bit more than just looking at you, Fletch.' I ran a teasing hand over his knee, up his thigh and ghosted across his crotch, laughing quietly when he gave a small shudder.

He sighed, 'I really wanted to get back before it got dark.'

'We will,' I said, looking outside in confusion, it was just after two in the afternoon so the sun wouldn't be setting for a couple more hours yet.

Fletcher switched on his emergency blinkers and pulled over to the side of the road, I watched him bemusedly. 'Is there a reason we're stopping?'

'Yeah,' he said as he put on the brake and unstrapped his seat belt, 'emergency.'

'What emergency would that be?'

He considered this with a tilt of his head as one hand reached out and cupped my boob past my unzipped coat and over my top. 'The very overwhelming need to fuck you.'

I should have laughed, I should have told him to keep driving. I had a feeling that was what he was expecting. Instead I said, 'Right here?' and his eyes became darker as he swallowed, pinching my nipple through the material.

'Yes,' he said hoarsely and I moved my hand back over his crotch again. I paused as I glanced in the back, I wasn't sure what type of car this was but it was tiny. Fletch glanced over his shoulder into the backseat too and frowned. 'Okay, maybe we'll have to wait.'

'Or…' I said as I slid down his zipper and guided his own hand to my sweats, 'we can just do something else.' I dipped my hand into his jeans and my breath hitched at the warmth of his dick filling my palm. I tugged him out and started slowly stroking him, Fletcher's breathing shifted in rhythm and his fingers slid beneath my waistband. He let out a growl when he remembered my lack of underwear and his fingers instead touched the dampness already gathering for him.

'Okay,' he panted as I worked him, 'but these need to be off. *Now.*'

I helped him tug my joggers down to my knees and spread my legs as much as I could in the limited space, laughing breathily when my knee knocked into the dash. Fletch's eyes didn't leave the motion of his hand against me, watching as he stroked his fingers along the sensitive flesh, parting me before dipping inside to flick against my clit. I gasped and he grinned, so I tightened my grip and began stroking him faster.

Satisfaction leapt inside me when he moaned my name,

until he thoroughly distracted me by slipping one and then a second finger deep inside me. I curled my hips under, encouraging him to move as I tried to concentrate on getting him off, on *winning*. Then it was a flurried rush of pants as our hips rose to meet the other's hand, neither wanting to come first but both needing to be pushed over the edge.

I moaned his name and he echoed my own back to me, his fingers moving in and out of me quickly until I clenched tightly around them with an *oh* to signal the end for me. My hips sank back down to the seat as he gently withdrew his fingers and licked them clean while I watched. Disappointment tinged my relaxation as I realised he'd made me come first – until I looked at him and found the evidence of his own ending still damp on his stomach.

'Who won?' I asked a little breathlessly and Fletcher grinned as he found a pack of tissues in his bag and used one to clean himself up quickly.

'I'd say we both did.'

I pulled up my joggers and Fletcher steered us back onto the road. One thing was for sure, I had never felt this confident or wild with a guy before – sex that wasn't sex outside? In a car? I liked that he made me feel confident enough to do those things with him. We passed another road marker and I smiled as Fletch intertwined our hands on his lap.

CHAPTER EIGHTEEN

SARA

I'd fallen asleep for the last leg of the drive back and had opened my eyes to the familiar early-evening sounds and lights of Anchorage. It turned out that Fletcher lived just about a twenty-minute drive from my place and I shot him an amused look at the realisation.

'If you live so close-by, why did it take you so long to pick me up the other day?'

He looked at me like the answer was obvious, 'Because I was scared to see you. You can be pretty fierce, gorgeous.'

I laughed as we pulled into a parking lot beneath his building, but by the time we'd walked up three flights of stairs to reach his apartment, I was no longer laughing. Then I spotted the elevator and waved in its direction indignantly while Fletch just grinned.

Everything seemed well-maintained in here, the corridor was gray and sleek, clearly new. Fletch was a lawyer for a big firm so him living somewhere a little snazzy was probably to be expected. He stopped outside of a door and I took the chance to admire his ass as we waited.

'Do you not have a key or something?' I asked as he knocked. His mouth opened but the door flew open before he could answer.

'Oh! Fletcher! You're early,' the woman behind the door said while I gaped.

'Sorry Ma'am, I hope I didn't interrupt anything,' Fletcher said and the lady waved him off with one well-wrinkled hand and then patted his face fondly, setting the grey curls pinned to her haid to quivering.

'Nonsense, I'll just get his stuff together. Won't be a moment,' she sent me a warm smile that I hesitantly returned and the second she was out of sight I turned to Fletcher expectantly.

'She's my neighbor,' he said, 'She sometimes watches Tib for me when I have to go out of town.'

Tib?

'Here we go,' a squirming ball of fur was thrust into my arms and a bag presumably containing food or something was shoved into Fletch's as the old woman returned. 'He's such a good boy, he's welcome any time.'

'Thank you again, Ms. Oscar. You call me if you need anything, you hear?'

There was a cat in my arms. Fletcher was a cat person.

It was dark grey and seemed to be ninety-percent fur. I'd never owned a pet and half-expected it to scratch me or bite me, but instead it peered up at me with curious eyes and licked the underside of my chin with a loud *meow*. An odd rumbling started up and I looked at Fletcher in a panic, 'There's something wrong with it – him – he's shaking!'

Fletcher laughed as he led me over to the black door opposite Ms. Oscar's, 'He's purring. He likes you.'

I looked down in shock and the cat patted me on the face with one paw, claws retracted, thankfully.

'You can set him down now,' Fletch said helpfully once we were inside, he took out a bowl and litter tray and arranged them in the hallway. I did as he instructed and then stared at Fletcher like he was an alien.

'You have a cat,' I said.

'I do,' he was trying not to laugh again, I could tell, until his brows furrowed. 'You're not like, allergic or anything are you?'

I wasn't. 'And if I was? Who would you keep, me or the cat?'

'Well that depends,' Fletch said as he prowled towards me and placed a hand on either side of my head, closing the front door. 'How often do you lick your ass and cough furballs?'

I laughed, the smell of his cologne making me dizzy in the best way, 'Never.'

'Then I'm afraid Tibs stays.'

We grinned at each other and when he stepped away I got my first proper look at his apartment. It was nice, hardwood floors ran through from the hall to what looked like a kitchen and the lounge area. It was mostly open plan but not as big or swanky as I had been nervously anticipating. I worked in marketing, it was fun but it didn't necessarily pay the big bucks.

Whereas Fletcher... he was a big-shot lawyer. He'd always seemed down-to-earth but I guess part of me had been a little scared that he might have a place big enough to *actually* have its own sex dungeon.

Fletcher smiled and held out a hand as he saw me taking in the place, 'Want a tour?'

I took his hand and said, 'I'd love that,' before kicking off my shoes at the door. He tugged me through to the lounge and surprisingly it was cosy. The walls were a warm brown and his sofa was a soft grey material that Tibs almost blended into, a thick rug sat over the wood and a large TV took up most of the space on the wall opposite the sofa.

'It's nice,' I said, truth be told, it looked like he'd probably put more effort into furnishing this place than I had mine.

'Don't sound so surprised,' he said, leading me over to peer around the breakfast bar inside the modern kitchen. Everything was so... shiny.

'Are you a clean freak?' I blurted, thinking with no short

amount of horror to all the mess I'd likely left lying around in the lodge.

'No,' he said with a shrug, 'I just cleaned before I left. Easy not to have mess when you haven't been here.'

Right. Easy. I thought back to the drawer-full of clothes I'd dumped onto my bed whilst packing and wanted to cry – it was a problem for another day though.

Fletch showed me his bathroom (large and equally shiny) and finally his bedroom, a small blush on his face as I caught a look at the positively massive bed that took up most of the space in there.

'Got it,' I said with a smirk, 'See, I told you before that you could tell a lot from someone's underwear drawer. What I failed to mention is that an orgy-sized bed tells a person even more.'

'I haven't hosted an orgy here,' he said, lips twitching and I gaped at him.

'But you have somewhere else?'

'What? No,' he laughed and turned, tugging me down onto the bed next to him. It was big but thankfully wasn't one of those horrifically dramatic four-poster beds or anything. In fact, Fletcher seemed... normal. 'So what do you want to do tonight?' he asked, the slight widening of his eyes telling me it wasn't a totally innocuous question.

'What I want...' I leaned in so my lips slightly brushed against his as I spoke, 'is Thai food.' I sat back and looked at him triumphantly as he blinked. 'I feel like I've eaten nothing but soup and pasta for the past few days and I need salt.'

'Sounds like a plan,' he stood and reached for his phone, scrolling for a second and then hitting dial as he walked back out into the hall and brought my bag into his bedroom. The man had *Thai Delight* saved to his contacts and for that I would have loved him alone.

My eyes bulged and Fletch looked at me in alarm, I waved him off as he began to talk to the restaurant. *Love?* Did I love Fletcher? Was that insane? I mean, true, the time we'd spent together down at the bay was more intense than casually dating for a few weeks but surely it was too soon to be –

'Sara? What do you want?' Ugh, his eyes were so blue. I quickly rattled off my usual order and went back to silently staring at him while his expression grew more worried at whatever mine held. He hung up and came back over to me, taking my hand and pressing a kiss to the back of it. 'Everything okay?'

I gave him a shaky smile and quick head bob that was probably wholly unconvincing, 'Yep! All good here, everything is just perfect.'

'Are you sure?' he said with a small frown, 'You look kind of pale and–'

'You know, I was just thinking that now we're… whatever we are, you can totally break bro-code and tell me what happened on that trip to San Francisco you and Rob took when you were in college.'

Successfully distracted, Fletch let a grin grow on his face as he recounted a tale of wild debauchery that would have appalled my mother.

'I can see why you're not allowed to tell that story,' I sank back onto his mattress and almost groaned, memory foam was the shit.

'Well, that's not even the best part.'

I cracked open an eye, 'It's not?'

Fletcher shook his head, his eyes dancing, 'When he woke up, he realised he actually knew the girl he was in bed with.'

'Oh?'

Fletch paused for dramatic effect, 'She was the Professor for his intro to bio class.'

My mouth popped open and Fletcher grinned broadly at having hooked me, 'Rob, my boring, straight-laced brother, slept with his teacher?'

'Yep.'

'Oh my God.'

We dissolved into laughter and Fletch flopped down onto

his back next to me, smiling as our eyes met. 'I'm glad you came here.'

'Me too.'

He opened his mouth and then shut it again and I tapped his arm until he opened it again, 'I'm glad we got snowed in together.'

I laughed, 'Me, too, Fletch.'

CHAPTER NINETEEN

SARA

The Thai food arrived and we consumed it like we hadn't seen food in days – which was sort of true. Tibs came and curled up on my lap and I sank my hand into his soft fur while Fletcher amused me with more stories about Rob. I guess he figured that since my brother had screwed us over, he had the right to dish a little dirt on the guy – not that I was complaining, I now had *so* much blackmail material on him.

We ended up back on the sofa and Fletch turned on the TV opposite, it was big enough that the light hurt my eyes at first. Fletcher stretched out a hand and rubbed my stomach, I let out a little *oof* of breath at the contact.

'Be careful,' I warned, 'I'm so full I might actually explode in a moment.'

His hand slid lower, 'Is this better?'

A smirk tugged at my mouth but I pushed it down, 'I don't think I can do anything too vigorous right now, Fletch.'

'That's okay gorgeous, you can stay exactly as you are for what I have in mind.'

'Oh? And what's that?'

Fletcher slid off of the sofa and onto his knees before me with a cocky smirk that had me instantly turned on, 'Dessert.' He pulled down my bottoms and I let out a sigh at the feel of his hands skating down my thighs, one leg pulled free of my clothes and then the other and he let out a pleased hum as he spread me wide.

I was aching for his touch but he seemed content to take his time, kissing up first one thigh and then the other, lingering around the sensitive crease of my leg until I impatiently tilted my hips. Craving contact.

'Considering how full you said you were, you definitely seem eager for more,' he said innocently as he pressed a finger into me and curled it in the way I liked, I pressed my hips down desperately.

'I'm just looking forward to when I get to have my way with you,' I said and he gave a low laugh.

'What do you think you're doing to me right now, gorgeous?'

He bent his head and I couldn't look away as his tongue brushed over my clit and his mouth found me, sucking gently until I couldn't hold my head up any longer. 'Fletcher,' I gasped as his finger slid in and out at a torturously slow pace while he tasted me like he was savouring it.

'Yes?' he asked, pulling away and licking his lips, when I said nothing else a hint of satisfaction spilled across his face and he bent back to my pussy eagerly.

I felt dizzy with pleasure as he worked me with his hands and tongue and I was close, so close. I opened my eyes and saw Tibs watching us.

'Fletcher.'

'Mm?'

'I can't do this,' I said around a breathy moan.

'What, this?' he asked, speeding up the pace of his fingers until I held on to the sofa, forgetting momentarily what I'd even been saying – why would I ever want him to stop? Then I opened my eyes again and remembered.

'No, no, I can't do this right now.'

Fletcher stopped and looked at me in alarm, his hair was mussed and his mouth was glistening and I tried so hard to focus my thoughts as he moved a hand to my knee, stroking it comfortingly. 'What's wrong?'

'I–' Maybe I was being stupid. But when I slid my gaze to the left again and found Tibs' unwavering stare I knew we needed to move. 'Your cat is watching us.'

For a second Fletcher just stared at me like I was speaking another language and then he burst out laughing, resting his head on my leg. I felt uncomfortably slippery as the mood started to evaporate, but then Fletcher stood and bent, scooping me up into his arms as I squealed.

'The bedroom it is, then,' He grinned and I pressed small kisses to his neck as we walked down the hallway to his bedroom. He placed me down onto the bed and I unbuckled his belt before he could step away, palming his dick through his jeans and delighting in the way his head fell back, exposing the long and golden column of his throat.

'You really don't have to–'

'I want to,' I said as I unzipped his fly, the sound raising goosebumps across my skin. His underwear was tight and dark blue and I looked up at him as I took him in my hand, feeling him jump against me. At the first touch of my lips he fisted his hands at his side and as I slid my tongue over his head he moaned my name.

There was something very powerful about knowing you could make someone completely undone with just your touch, and I felt that moving through me as I took him deep into my mouth, giving a small gasp of pleasure when his hand found my breast and began squeezing it.

'You are just–' his eyes were glazed as they looked down at me, he licked his lips as he watched me take him in again, increasing the suction until he swayed lightly on his feet and buried his hand in my hair to stay upright.

He tasted salty and smokey on my tongue and I drew back with one last flick of my tongue before this could be over – I wasn't done with him yet. Fletcher brought his mouth to mine and I sighed into him. He took a step away from the bed and drew his shirt over his head, my eyes followed the bunching and smoothing of his muscles as he stripped for me. This time was different though, this time, I would get to touch.

His underwear fell to the floor and a tingle of anticipation made me feel a little nervous, despite the fact that we'd already had sex at the lodge, this felt like a step further.

'You don't know how many times I've thought about this the past month, having you here in my bed,' his voice was husky and suddenly I felt like I couldn't wait another second, needing him inside me.

'I probably do, because I've been thinking about the same thing since the wedding.'

A smug look overtook his face and I grinned, pulling my top up and over my head, leaving myself entirely bare for him. Fletch stopped and looked at me, a flush spread across my skin as he closed the few steps between us and climbed onto the bed.

'Bend over,' he ordered and I obeyed, getting on o my hands and knees. He moved behind me and took a hold of my wrists, sliding my hands further out so my nipples brushed the bed cover and then moving his hands back to rest on my hips. 'Open your legs.' He gave a low groan when I did and I knew he was as desperate as me in that moment. 'Touch yourself,' these words were softer, but still demanding and I moved one of my hands down and began to stroke my clit while he watched. 'Good, I'm going to make you come for me now Sara.'

I moaned his name and didn't have time to prepare before he was filling me, stretching me out as I continued to press my fingers against myself. 'Fletcher,' I panted and thrust my hips back against him, begging for more, and his voice was hoarse when he spoke.

'God, I love the way you move.' He drew back and then pushed into me again, harder, faster, until my hips were rolling helplessly into his and the only sounds were our moans and our bodies meeting. Fletcher cursed as I tightened around him,

'Not yet.' Cupping me under my thighs, he gently withdrew before laying back and tugging me on top of him. 'I want you to ride me until you come, Sara. I want you to scream for me when you do.'

I let my legs fall wide and felt him near my entrance as I situated myself, sinking down onto him in a way that was altogether deeper and somehow *more*. I drew my legs up slightly and ground against him, lifting myself and bouncing, loving the way he shuddered underneath my body, the way his hands gripped my ass. I increased the pace but it wasn't enough, I needed it to be faster, I wanted more of him. I leaned forward and pressed our lips together, letting him take over as he held me to his chest and fucked me until I was shaking, shouting out his name.

When the sweat had started to cool on our bodies, he moved me off to his side and stroked my hair. I smiled at him and he smiled back. It was strange, with Rob I felt our age difference so keenly, but I was twenty-seven and Fletch was thirty-two and it seemed easy as breathing for us.

'Do you mind that I'm a bit younger than you?' I asked sleepily and Fletcher's eyebrows scrunched together.

'Not at all, I don't even notice the gap. Why, does it bother you?'

'No, I was just thinking how it's strange that I can always feel the difference when I'm with Rob even though he's only a few years older.'

'That's because Rob is thirty-going-on-seventy.' I laughed because it was true, I often felt like my brother was a little too serious. 'Though, to be fair that's pretty common when you're forced to grow up maybe a little too fast. You were what, nine, when your dad died?'

'Yeah,' I said quietly, 'I feel bad though because I just don't remember him the way Rob can, you know? Ugh, let's not talk about my brother right now.'

'Okay,' Fletcher said gently, tucking a strand of red hair behind my ear, 'what *do* you want to talk about?'

'You,' I said with a smile that spelled mischief, 'let's start with girlfriends shall we?'

CHAPTER TWENTY

FLETCHER

Sara had grilled me on everything from my past girlfriends (none that were serious), my favourite colour (blue, which she had declared 'boring') and my favourite thing about my job (was it wrong of me to say the money?). I'd run her a bath and left her to soak while I did something I really didn't want to do.

'Hey man,' I sighed when Rob picked up, 'I saw I had a missed call from you and just wanted to check-in.'

'Does Sara know you're calling me?'

'Not yet,' I said carefully, 'She's in the bath right now.' An awkward silence descended and I blew out a long breath. 'Look, I know she's your sister but–'

'I'm happy for you both. If I wasn't okay with you two, why would I have gone to all that trouble to set you up, only to have it blow back in my face?'

Point. 'Okay, yeah, true. I'm still mad at you though and I know Sara is too.'

There was an emotion in Rob's voice Fletcher hadn't heard before, guilt? 'Do you think she'd talk to me if I came by to apologise?'

'I don't think she feels that you have that word in your vocabulary.'

'Please Fletch, just... don't tell her I'm coming okay? If

you do, she'll leave.' No, it wasn't guilt, it sounded closer to desperation.

'Okay, but if she asks you to leave it's not my fault.'

'I get it, but I can't leave things like this between us. My sister is stubborn as all hell and she'd easily hold onto this forever if I let her.'

'I'm making no promises.'

'I know, but thank you.'

Rob hung up in that way that always annoyed me, it was abrupt and signaled *I have better things to do now than talk to you*. I loved him like a brother, but then again, I supposed nobody could annoy you quite like family.

'Can you believe him?' I murmured to Tibs as I scratched him under the chin, he was purring in figure eights by my feet so I knew what it was he wanted. 'Come on then, let's feed you.'

Once my cat had been satisfied, I went to check on Sara and laughed when I walked in on her dozing in the bath. 'Hey,' I said softly, touching her arm. 'Why don't we get you out of here and into something cosy?'

She murmured something about the bath in the lodge as she got out and I made soothing *Mms* and *Ohs* as she spoke and I dried her off with one of the towels from the radiator.

I could get used to this, I thought and that didn't scare me as much as I'd once thought it would.

'Have you given any more thought into talking to Rob?' I asked Sara the next day as she walked into the lounge and her nose wrinkled adorably. 'Don't be mad, but I had a missed call from him so I actually spoke to him yesterday. He seems genuinely sorry.'

Sara shook her head, her hair flying about in agitation, 'He went behind our backs to meddle in our love life. He should be more than sorry.'

I sighed, Sara was as stubborn as her brother, 'Okay, well, clearly you hold grudges. Question: if he hadn't interfered, would you even be talking to me right now?'

It was quiet for a moment while she thought about it and then she slumped down next to me on the sofa, pressing herself into my side. 'I guess I see your point. But that doesn't make what he did okay.'

'You're right, it doesn't,' I reasoned, holding up one hand, 'but I think he knows that. Besides, without Rob's sneakiness you wouldn't have had the opportunity to come twice already this morning.'

She laughed at what I was sure was a smug expression on my face, 'Ugh, let's not mention Rob and orgasms in the same sentence please.' I laughed and she nibbled her lip before turning to me and staring deep into my eyes. 'I am grateful that he brought you into my life though, I've had the most incredible–'

'Satisfying,' I cut in and she rolled her eyes at me.

'–*satisfying*, few days and I honestly don't remember the last time I enjoyed myself this much. Not even just in like, a sex way. Plus,' a smile flirted with her mouth and I dropped my gaze to her lips, 'it's nice having someone around who can cook. I burn water.'

I leaned in and pressed a quick kiss to her cheek and then her mouth, 'You can't be that bad.'

'I take it Rob never told you about the time we tried to do Thanksgiving at my place then. We had to call the fire department in the end.'

She was utterly ridiculous and gorgeous and I loved the way her eyes got all wide when she recounted her crazy antics. 'The fire department?'

'Yeah, that was one inedible turkey after I'd had my way with it.'

We both curled up in laughter and I kissed her on her smile, she pulled me closer and my fingers slid into her soft hair. Her hands ran across my chest and I sighed, wondering how quickly I could carry her to my bedroom and have her naked, when there was a knock on the door.

I was only expecting one person and I groaned, God her brother had terrible timing. I smoothed Sara's hair with one hand as I strode to unlock the door for my best friend.

'Hi,' I said, my eyes running over him with concern. His hair was mussed and there was a faint shadow of beard on his jaw that said more about his mental state than possibly anything else could have. 'Are you okay?'

'I'm fine. Can I come in?'

Sara rounded the corner, 'Who's at– Oh.' Then her eyes took in Rob and I saw the same worry in them that was reflected in mine, but she clearly wasn't going to let this go without making him sweat a little first. 'Rob.'

I gestured for him to come in and then headed to the kitchen, tossing Rob a beer that he promptly set on the side atop a coaster. I hadn't even known I owned coasters, so I wasn't sure where he'd found one. I briefly entertained myself with the thought that he had resorted to carrying them around with him to maintain order.

'Sara, I'm sorry. You too, Fletch. I shouldn't have messed with you both and tried to manipulate you into getting together. Even if it worked.' Rob's fingers drummed at the arm of the sofa and his eyes darted around the room. This was clearly hard from him, I'd seen him more relaxed in a street brawl than he was right now.

Sara sighed, 'I'm grateful to have Fletcher in my life, but I wish you'd just come and spoken to us. I know it's not something we do nearly often enough,' she reached out and took his hand, stilling the frantic movement of his fingers, 'but there's still time to change that.'

'You mean that?' Rob asked, a strangely wet look in his eye as he stared at his sister and I cleared my throat, feeling like maybe I should leave when Sara glanced at me briefly and I could tell she wanted me to stay.

'Of course! I don't hate you Rob, all I want is for you to try to remember I'm not a child any more. You don't need to lecture me, or criticise me, or turn every failure into a teachable moment. Just... be my brother.' Sara's jaw was clenched and I wanted to ease away the strain for her, for them both.

'I'll do better,' Rob said, relief evident on his face, and then he lurched forward, scooping her into a giant hug that had her shooting a *What The Fuck* look at me when he released her.

'I will too,' she said and this time her smile was soft, all was clearly forgiven. They both looked to me and I blinked.

'Oh, er, yeah, sure, me too.'

'No, dumbass, your phone is ringing.' Sara looked like she wasn't sure if she wanted to tweak my nose or kiss me and I gave a small chuckle as I pulled my phone free of my pocket.

'It's Providence calling,' I said in confusion and Rob and Sara shared a worried look. 'Hello?'

'Hi, I'm looking for a Fletcher Harris on behalf of Robert Bridges?'

'Speaking and Rob is right here with me. Is everything okay?' My heart was pounding and my mouth felt dry, pretty much everyone I was close to in Anchorage that could have me down as an emergency contact was sitting right here. That only left one person. Tanya.

'We have a Mrs. Tanya Bridges here and we were unable to get hold of the primary emergency contact number. Could we speak to Robert?'

I wordlessly passed the phone over to Rob and he looked stricken, his face paling further until his dark eyes looked black against his pallor.

'Rob Bridges speaking,' he said and then he bit his lip, nodding even though the person on the other end of the line couldn't see him. 'I'll be there as soon as I can.'

Sara had her hand on her brother's arm as he hung up and

I could see the whiteness of her knuckles from where I was sitting. 'What's going on?'

'It's Tan,' Rob said, his voice a little faint and his eyes unfocused. He shook his head and clenched his fists. 'They said the power went out at the lodge and when she turned it back on there was a spark in the fusebox that got her. They've taken her to Emergency but they wouldn't tell me exactly why over the phone.'

Sara jumped up, spooking Tibs from the corner of the chair and causing him to run into the kitchen where he peered balefully out at us. 'Okay, we'll take the rental and we'll go and find out what's going on.' She took Rob in a tight hug, 'I'm sure she's fine.'

CHAPTER TWENTY-ONE

SARA

We made it to the Emergency room in just under fifteen minutes and Rob was sweating profusely by the time I pulled up. I had been allowed to drive because they needed my, quote, 'oh-shit' driving, whatever that meant. Either way, we'd brushed past two red lights in the nick of time and Fletcher was holding onto the handle of the car door like he was scared it was going to fly open.

'Now I've seen you drive first hand, I can understand why nobody is that comfortable with you doing it,' he muttered as we pushed through the doors and Rob led the way to the reception desk. He was a doctor and I guessed all the hospital layouts were likely very similar, because he located it much quicker than I probably would have.

The red-haired receptionist didn't look too keen on helping and moved at a snail's pace, clicking her tongue as she waited for an ancient-looking computer to load the necessary documents. She checked Rob's ID and then mine and Fletcher's for good measure. Rob was allowed to go and see her but we had to wait by the reception for updates.

My brother hurried off to find his wife and Fletcher and I claimed seats in the eye-line of the hallway so we could see him return. My thoughts were spinning as I remembered what Rob said about the electric box – we should have warned them, or reported it or done something to prevent this from happening. Because now Tanya was sitting in a bed somewhere down the corridor maybe, hurt or–

Fletcher took my hand and squeezed it, 'I can literally hear your mind working right now. Take a breath. Tanya is going to be fine.'

'Do you think we did this?' I wrung my hands together and jiggled my knee up and down. 'If she got here at the same time as Rob got to your place that means they must have airlifted her or something. Which means it's bad.'

'We don't know that,' Fletcher said soothingly, rubbing small circles into my back until I could breathe normally again. 'And the fusebox was clearly faulty, but we had no way of knowing she would go down there and get hurt. Don't put this on your shoulders, gorgeous.'

We waited for another half hour before Rob emerged from down the hall, Fletch keeping up a solid stream of soothing chatter the whole time. My brother looked simultaneously like he'd had the fright of his life and that a weight had been lifted from his shoulders.

I jumped up from my seat and walked quickly towards him. The waiting room was mostly empty but I didn't want to make a scene by running. 'Is she okay?'

Rob's smile lit up his whole face, 'She's perfect.'

Relief welled up and I felt my shoulders finally move down from around my ears. 'How comes they airlifted her here if she's perfect?'

'Well,' Rob said and there was a definite hint of mischief to the spark in his eyes, 'it seems my lovely wife has been keeping secrets too.'

'Rob, I swear to God if you don't hurry up and tell me–'

'Tanya's pregnant!' He burst out, the grin on his face stretching so wide it literally was almost ear-to-ear. 'She found out just before our trip. The shock from the fusebox was pretty nasty and she had some bleeding that the doctors were concerned about. Apparently there was an accident on the Highway so they flew her instead just to make sure the baby was okay.'

A smile broke out across my face and I jumped on the spot excitedly, 'I'm going to be an aunt! Oh my God, you're going to be a *Dad*!'

Fletcher slapped Rob on the back, an equally pleased grin overtaking the worry that had been there.

'I'm so glad she's okay. Will they be releasing her soon?' I couldn't wait to see her and squeal over this together. 'How far along is she?'

'Literally just over two months, they want to keep her the night to observe her but they think everything looks good.'

I smirked, 'I'm telling Mom you had sex before marriage.'

Rob laughed, 'I think she'll be so happy about grandkids that she wouldn't care if the baby had three feet and came out singing.'

'Okay,' Fletcher said with a deep laugh that had my heart singing, 'you're getting delirious now. Get back to your woman and call us if you need anything. You can crash at mine if you need.'

'I'm probably going to stay here with Tan, but thanks man.' Rob smiled softly and suddenly looked very tired, I brushed a quick kiss across his cheek.

'Congratulations,' I murmured as I took him in a hug. 'Give my love to Tanya, please?'

Rob nodded and gave a smile to Fletch as he strolled back along the corridor.

'Wow, what a whirlwind,' I said as we watched him walk away. 'I can't believe she's pregnant. Now I get to be the cool aunt I've always wanted to be.'

'Just as long as you don't attempt to drive that kid about,' Fletcher said with a grin and I swatted him on the arm.

'You had to ruin the moment huh?' I smiled and moved closer, touching his arm gently. 'Thank you for being there and for keeping me somewhat calm. I'm not so good with hospitals and well, I just think you're so amazing and I love you and –' I froze. No. *Tell me I didn't say that aloud.* One look at Fletcher's face was all I needed to know, and worse, he was still silent. His beautiful blue eyes were completely round and his mouth had popped open.

I felt hot and then cold and the saliva in my mouth seemed to double as we both stood there, staring at each other. *Should I take it back? Laugh like it was a joke?* I wasn't sure I was capable of making any sound at all right then. *Stupid idiot, Sara! You finally find a guy you like and you tell him you love him after only being official for like three days?* No wonder Rob had thought I was such a mess – turned out, he was right.

Fletcher's mouth opened and closed, like he was searching for the words, but it didn't matter. There's only ever one response you want to hear when you tell someone you love them for the first time and shocked silence definitely wasn't it.

I span, dashing for the exit like my life depended on it without any real idea of where the hell I was going. I stumbled out of the main entrance and the cold air hit me like a balm, clearing my head but allowing the sting of rejection to settle in. I'd told Fletcher I loved him and he hadn't said it back. Hadn't said anything at all, and I wasn't sure which was worse.

Oh God, this was so humiliating. I spotted a taxi rank off to the side and quickly dashed over, feeling my breaths starting to rasp in faster and tears starting to cloud my eyes. There was a vaguely startled-looking driver sitting and waiting in the front seat, jumping as I threw open the door and bundled myself in. Was that Fletcher calling my name? *No. You're imagining it. You said I love you and he said…* Nothing. He'd said nothing.

'Do you want to go somewhere?' the driver asked hesitantly and I released a loud breath as I tried to quiet my tears with little success. They started pouring down my face as I looked at the driver, I offered him a curt nod and the tight set to my mouth clearly told him not to ask.

'Can you take me to Ninth by Delaney?'

'Sure, no problem.' He had a sort of grandfatherly air about him and I was relieved to have climbed into a car with a half decent person and not some ass who was going to pepper me with questions the whole way home. *Fuck.* I didn't even have any of my stuff. Luckily I kept a spare key in the fake hanging basket by the door, but I hated sticking my hand in there for fear of spiders.

How was I supposed to come back from this? Fletcher wasn't just some guy off the street that I'd met and fallen for – he was my brother's best friend, he was in my life for good one way or another. I groaned, *Rob.* Fletch would tell Rob, obviously, and then Rob would inevitably tell our mother, leading to at least four phone calls a day while she 'checks-in"– which was basically just her asking how I was and if I was okay with increasing worry as the day went on.

I was going to have to move and change my name. No, I needed to move to a convent and take a vow of silence so nobody would have to be on the receiving end of another impromptu and ill-timed *I love you* ever again. Or, well, at least not from me anyway.

Fuck, I hoped this taxi took apple pay because I had zero cash on me right now, what with my wallet being with rest of my bags at Fletcher's and it wasn't like I could go back there. Goodbye favourite fuzzy socks, goodbye special facial exfoliator brush that I paid $40 for.

We passed Delaney park and I directed the old man to my place, thanking him when we pulled up out front. 'Do you take apple pay? If not, I'll have to run inside and find some cash for you.'

The man looked startled, 'Oh, I'm not a taxi driver.'

I stared at him for a moment before bursting into laughter. 'Very funny, how much do I owe you?'

'Nothing, dear,' he said, reaching back and petting my hand gently before letting go. 'You just go ahead and feel better soon. I hope whoever you were visiting is okay.'

Oh. Oh no. This was a new low. I'd accidentally kidnapped someone's actual grandpa and he thought I was crying over a dying relative rather than some guy. I shook my head in disbelief as I climbed out and gave the guy a friendly wave through my sniffling.

I just needed to get inside, put on my baggiest and comfiest tee and then cry on my sofa for the rest of the night. I patted through my pockets when I got to the door, crying harder when I remembered for the second time that all I had on me were the keys to the rental car and my cell phone. *Great, you also left Fletcher stranded because you have the keys to the car.* Judging by the utter shock on his face, I was willing to bet that he was probably still stood in the hospital waiting room. Then he'd tell Rob what I'd done and that would be it, I'd never hear the end of it.

Like, yes, maybe I was an idiot, but I couldn't help the way I felt. *Yes but you didn't need to blurt it out so soon.*

My place was dark and a little cold as I walked in, the key in my hand was probably covered in cobwebs but I refused to look at it, instead I placed it down on the window ledge and went immediately to wash my hands.

It felt… empty. I'd only been at Fletcher's for a couple of nights but I already missed his absurdly gigantic bed and his grey furball. I'd screwed up and it hurt to admit it.

Maybe I'd overreacted, maybe this wasn't the death knell for relationships that I thought it was. He had to love me one day, right? So, we could just ignore that I'd said it and… and have it be the elephant in every room and conversation.

I sighed as I kicked off my shoes. On the bright side, at least I didn't have to unpack.

CHAPTER TWENTY-TWO

FLETCHER

I just think you're so amazing and I love you –
She loved me. Sara Bridges. Loved... me?
My heart was pounding like it wanted to jump right out of my chest and meet hers, my tongue felt too big for my mouth and, *fuck,* was I sweating? I'm pretty sure I was sweating, the heat flashing through me increased the longer Sara's eyes held mine and I wanted to grin, to sweep her into my arms, to kiss her, to laugh – except I couldn't do that last one, out of context it would have looked really bad.

So why wouldn't my damned mouth work?

Sara was growing paler and still all I could do was stare at her stupidly, this beautiful, crazy woman who, for some reason, loved *me*. I opened my mouth but no sound came out, my eyes were beginning to hurt from how wide they'd become but panic began to make my breaths burn and Sara's eyes became wet and her mouth curled in that way that meant she was holding back tears.

Before I could get my body back under some semblance of control, Sara turned and ran straight back down the corridor towards the main entrance. Adrenaline made my stomach churn and I knew that if I didn't catch her, I would lose her for good this time. She'd made herself vulnerable to me again and I'd been an idiot... again. I just hadn't expected it. I was pretty sure I'd been half in-love with her ever since she threw my jumper at me in the snow but I'd known for sure when she hit her head in the basement – those had been some of the scariest few minutes of my life, seeing her prone and utterly silent on the floor.

A breath juddered out of me and I walked a few halting steps, shock making my body slow at first. I made it to the main entrance and dashed out. Red hair whipped about in the air and I caught another flash of it slipping inside a deep blue car .

'Sara!' I called as I ran, but she either didn't want to talk to me or didn't hear me. But I didn't care either way, she had to be heading home and this time I wasn't walking away or moping. I was going to get her back, because *I loved her too*, damn it.

I frantically patted down my pockets as I made my way to the rental car at a brisk pace. *Crap. Sara has the keys*. I groaned, throwing my arms up to cradle my head as I stared at the sky, it was threatening to rain and I spared a thought to how terrifying an experience it would have been in the car with Sara on slick roads. It had been bad enough driving to the hospital, I was fairly sure Sara had been a racing driver in a previous life or something with the way she'd taken the turns. The tires had screeched and I could have sworn the back wheels had lost contact with the road several times. Rob had called it her 'oh-shit' driving and to be fair, it made a lot of sense. I could have got us here safer, but nowhere near as fast.

Luckily, I had my wallet and was able to snag a taxi after only ten or so minutes waiting. I wanted to go straight to Sara's, but decided instead to go home and collect her stuff. I would have loved for to come back to mine with me, but she was likely already at home and getting her to even let me in was going to be challenge enough.

I thanked and paid the driver quickly when we pulled up to my apartment building about twenty minutes later. There had been some traffic and every second of delay had made my hands clench tighter together. At least Rob had driven my truck down from the lodge after it had been fixed, it was a small comfort though. I knew as soon as I got in it that Sara would be at the forefront of my thoughts, the way she'd looked curled up in the leather seats as she'd tried to focus on her book, her fruity scent filling the air. She was already on my mind now as I dashed up the three flights of stairs, remembering her disgust when she'd realised there'd been an elevator, I snorted but my amusement faded quickly. I couldn't lose her now.

Tibs *meow*ed loudly as I walked in and I bent to give him a quick scratch under his chin before collecting Sara's stuff. Somehow, in the space of two nights, she'd managed to spread things out everywhere – her hairbrush on top of my drawers, her toothpaste by the sink, a book on the sofa, little touches of her that I collected up and replaced into her bags before crashing back out the door again.

My truck purred to life and I breathed a sigh of relief, now for the hard part – convincing the woman who loved me that I loved her back.

The journey to her apartment was a blur and I took it as a good sign that the earlier traffic had cleared up. Except, I hadn't had nearly enough time to figure out what I was going to say to her yet. I didn't want to wing it but I thought maybe I'd know what to say when I saw her. Or I'd freeze up again. *No, that was just the shock. You've got this.*

I took several deep breaths as I pulled into her driveway. I was sweating again, I didn't get it, I'd *never* been a nervous sweater – just another way that Sara had turned my life upside down. Should I play something on the aux to calm myself down first? I needed to be at my best and could have used a little *Adele* right about now.

I winced, the aux was in the rental. *I guess there's no more delaying.* I pushed open the car door, humming Rolling in the Deep under my breath to hype myself up a bit as I rang the bell.

No answer.

I rang it again and then realised I'd left her stuff in my car, should I go and get it? What if she opened the door while I was gone and thought it was a prank? I hesitated but when no footsteps approached I jogged back to the car and pulled out her bags. She had to answer. If I had to annoy her into it then I would. Now I understood why the guys in movies used boomboxes – if you had to annoy someone into talking to you, it was better to serenade them with music than the sound of a doorbell.

I placed her bags on the doorstep and leaned on the bell, a mixture of apprehension and dread curling in my throat when I heard the rapid patter of footsteps and Sara opened the door. Her red hair was in disarray and she had chocolate ice-cream smeared on her mouth, a grey tee fell to her mid-thigh and her hands curled on the hem when she saw me at the door.

Her eyes dropped to the bags on the front step and her voice was croaky when she spoke, 'Oh, you brought my stuff back. Thanks, that was nice of you.'

My heart ached at the puffiness of her eyes and the wetness clinging to her lashes. God damn I was an idiot. 'Of course. I'm sorry, I should have brought flowers or whisky or maybe a rifle, I don't know, but please let me in so we can talk?'

She bit her lip, indecision clearly warring within her as her body still blocked the doorway even as her eyes scanned me from head to toe. 'What is there to talk about?'

Time to wing it, I guess. I looked into her face and took a slow step forward, she stayed where she was and I felt my hands loosen. I cupped her face, 'How about how I'm the biggest idiot to have ever walked the Earth? Or how ridiculously lucky I am to have someone like you in my life?' I took a breath, looked deep into her bright green eyes and said what I needed to. 'Someone who loves me just as much as I love them.'

In another situation I might have laughed at how wide her eyes became.

'You love me too?' she whispered the words as if worried that I might freeze again and I wiped the chocolate from her face with my thumb, bringing it to my lips and tasting it.

'Yes,' I said, moving closer so that I was almost inside the door, our bodies were so close I could feel the warmth rising off of her as I lowered my lips to hers, 'I love you, Sara.'

She sighed against my mouth and I let my tongue twine around hers, revelling in her moan as I swept her up and into my arms. Her legs wrapped around my waist and I would have taken her right then and there if not for the fact that the door was still open, her bags outside, and goosebumps were running up and down her calves. I stroked a hand over one leg and slid her down my body and back onto the floor.

I grabbed her bags and closed the door, setting them down on the floor before I turned back to her. The smile on her face made my breath catch. I took her hands in mine, 'Tell me again.'

She smiled as I leaned in for another kiss, 'I love you, Fletcher.'

'No more running,' I mumbled against her and she gave a laugh that warmed me right to my bones.

'No more running,' she agreed and I lost myself in our kisses and the feel of her skin.

EPILOGUE

SARA

Fletcher laughed as Cammie threw a toy at my head while I tried to wipe milk-puke off of my top. I held the squirming baby out to Fletcher in desperation and he took her with no complaints. Rob and Tanya had gone on a weekend break, leaving their six-month-old daughter in my – okay, Fletch's – capable hands. Rob had needed to drag Tanya away after I'd made an off-hand comment about babies and alcohol, I wasn't really that stupid, I knew they couldn't drink until they were at least like, fifteen. Rob had rolled his eyes at me but smiled. A lot had changed. Most of it good.

The truth was, I had very little experience with babies. They were cute, but I hadn't realised just how *sticky* they could be. Or how prone to puke. Fletcher took everything in stride, how he didn't worry about their floppy heads and tiny little bodies, I had no clue. Every time Cammie was in my arms I had an existential crisis at the fragility of her squishy body. Fletcher said that was my maternal instincts but it felt a lot more like anxiety.

Either way, I was much more prepared to be Fun Aunt Sara than Responsible Aunt Sara. That was why Fletcher had been a godsend. He'd moved in with me just before Cammie was born, I adored his apartment but my place was simply bigger. Tibs had adjusted well, though he wasn't quite sure what to make of the baby yet, prodding at Cammie's chubby hands with one careful paw and running away before she could get a hold of his tail or ears.

Cammie cooed in Fletcher's arms and his eyes were soft as he rocked her in whooshing movements from side to side, making her giggle in delight. At least we knew at this early age that she was already more fun than Rob – though he'd lightened up a lot since Tanya had become pregnant, he'd even laughed when I'd said that to him. Shocking.

Our Mom had been thrilled with Cammie's arrival and I knew she was sad to have missed out on babysitting her this weekend but Rob had declared it was my turn and I had nervously agreed.

Things between Fletcher and I had been amazing. Almost too good to be true, sometimes I found myself waiting for the other shoe to drop and I'd discover he had some weird hobby that would drive us apart. Yet so far, we were far too similar for our own good – except for music, he was a staunch ballad fan where I'd rather listen to... anything else really.

Oddly enough, we all looked back on the lodge fondly – though I wouldn't be going back any time soon – Tanya had even debated calling the baby Mack after the bay. Rob had talked her out of that one by flying her to Paris. I guessed he'd really hated the name.

Cammie had her head snuggled beneath Fletch's chin, her dark hair looking sweet with small curls springing up at the back and I tugged on one lightly as I went over to stand next to them.

'Surely it's time for her nap now?' I asked somewhat desperately. I definitely wasn't ready for one of these sweet monsters, but the practicing was definitely appealing.

Fletcher sent me a dark grin, 'You want one then?' he asked and I shook my head quickly.

'Er no, just you.' He looked a little hurt and I hastened to correct myself, 'I mean, I don't know, maybe one day or something but –'

A hand covered my mouth, 'Shhh,' Fletcher said. 'She's asleep.' He walked into the second bedroom that was currently serving as a nursery during Cammie's stay. He walked back out empty handed a moment later and pressed a kiss to my cheek.

'Fletch,' I began but he sighed.

'*Sara*,' a smile spread on his lips, 'I love you. It's fine. I can wait.'

'What if I don't ever want kids?' I whispered and Fletch stroked a hand across my cheek.

'Then Tibs will have a lot of brothers and sisters in his future,' Fletcher chuckled and I felt any tension in me melt away. 'Besides, we can get very good at practicing,' his teeth nipped at my ear and I hissed in a breath, 'just in case.'

I laughed quietly as he pulled me towards our bedroom, 'I'm okay with that.'

'I thought you might be,' he said, closing the door softly behind us.